KARMA

Candy Ain't Always Sweet

LeJune Papillon

ISBN -13: 978-1463787486
ISBN-10:   1463787480

Edited By: Papillon Books

First Edition

KARMA
Candy Ain't Always Sweet

LeJune Papillon

Dedication

This book is dedicated to my parents, Robert and Orretta Turner who believed I could fly before I ever knew I could walk. I know they are smiling in heaven as I spread my wings.

Acknowledgement

God is Awesome.

I would like to thank everyone who has supported my crazy ideas from the beginning, and those who really believed me when I first said, "I'm going to write a book".

I would like to thank my friends and family.

Special Thanks to my lifelong support team, June, Robert C., Anthony, Patrick, Travis and Lil' Ant.

The Book Club With Out a Name

Thank you if you are reading this book and supporting the adventures of Ms. Gwen, Karma and Janeese.

Ms. Gwen

Karma & Janeese

Leon's Club

Mr. Samuel's

Graduation Day

Charlie Ain't My Daddy

T-Bone

Ms. Mocha Latte

I Kissed a Girl

A Prayin' Woman?

Work the Plan

It's No Longer a Situation

A Real Man

We Goin' To College

Club Excite

"Dumbassory" Is a Felony

Ms. Gwen's Picnic

1

MS. GWEN

They all call me Ms. Gwen, but my God given name is Gwendolyn Evalese Anderson. I am fifty-seven years old and I look damn good for my age, but baby believe me when I say it has not been an easy road. I was lucky enough to make it through the rough years with only two babies of my own but in reality I have had thousands of babies. I am what is known as the matriarch. I am the matriarch of this community. I have lived in this community all of my life. I have seen people come and people go. I have wiped some runny noses and cleaned some funky diapers. I have seen these babies shot down in the streets. You name it. Ms. Gwen has seen it and done most of it too. Chile listen, Ms. Gwen has had many men, and all kinds and trust me I can spot a no good man when I see his snake ass slithering up.

That reminds me of that damn Charlie. Charlie was dark as a night at home alone with the electricity off. He was one dark piece of chocolate. Now I ain't complaining about that cause Ms. Gwen love her some chocolate honey. Charlie had a certain way about him. The young folks call it swag. Well when I first saw Mr. Dark Night walking toward me at the tavern I almost peed my panties, but I remembered I wasn't wearing none. I squeezed that Jack Daniels on the rocks like it was my pillow. He just had something about him and oooo weeeee... I liked it. So Charlie was bringin his swag right by me and I ain't ashamed to say, I wanted some of that—SWAG. It was real tight up in Kozy's tavern that night. He had to squeeze past me to get through. Just when he was about to squeeze through, I stood my hot ass up and he had to rub it to get through. I had on a short black skirt with a bow positioned right above my ass crack; my ass was the present that night. I already told you I wasn't wearin' any panties, just in case something jumped off, you know. I had on a sheer black tank top with my very best push up bra and chile you know I was wearing some four inch, red, come and get it pumps. Charlie was smelling good and lickin his lips like he had just finished a good ol' piece of fried chicken. He was so dark all I could see was his eyes and his teeth, but I liked what I saw, and what I felt. As Mr. Charlie was squeezing past me he put his hands on my waist. I turned around, smiled and said, "Excuse me mister, but is that a gun you packing? I ain't lookin for no trouble honey." He smiled again. And damn he had some pretty white teeth. He said "No baby, but if I need to frisk you we are in the perfect position for it." He said, "Hi sexy, my name is Charlie". I turned around and he was so close. The girls were sitting up so high, I thought for sure one of my nipples was gonna pop right in his mouth. I cleared my throat and said, "Hi I'm Ms. Gwen." Charlie said, "What you drinkin' Ms. Gwen?" I said, Jack on the rocks", but it don't look like I'm gonna need the rocks tonight. He ran his sweet tongue along the side of my neck and the rest is history. Baybee, that night, before it was all said and done, Charlie discovered that I had left my panties at the house, and let's just say, his swag was tight!

Little did I know but this was the overlay for the under play. I laid and played right along for about four months. I saw Charlie day in and day out. It was me and it was Charlie. I was starting to catch some feelings for this dark man. We went everywhere and did everything. Some of the neighbors would see me alone and yell from across the street, "Hey Girl, Where is Charlie?" Everybody liked Charlie; he had that kind of personality. I was enjoying the ride and didn't want to get off, but when we found out that I was pregnant,

Mr. Dark Chocolate melted away. I ain't heard from his sweet smelling raggedy ass since. He left me with a lot of memories, a hot ass and of course KARMA. That's when I first learned that my weakness was for chocolate... but I also learned that candy ain't always sweet.

I had Karma without Charlie. When I first saw her face I just cried and cried. She looked like that damn Charlie. I cried so much I lost all of the baby weight. Karma was a combination of my caramel skin tone and Charlie's dark chocolate tone. She had a smooth, mocha latte kind of color. I knew right then that she was going to be a beautiful girl. Although my heart was hurting, I was so happy and so proud of what me and Charlie created together.

KARMA

When I thought about how Charlie had sucked me in with his pretty white teeth and that damn swag, and how he left me just as soon as he took over my life and my heart, I was angry. I named my baby KARMA Marie Anderson. I named her Karma because I didn't want my baby to have to put up with the same shit that I did all these years with these trifling ass men and women. They are all haters. I will raise her to deal with things as they happen. There will be no turn the other cheek and no forgiveness for these suckers. That didn't work for me. I can save her some pain. If she just listen to Ms. Gwen, she gon be alright.

My sweet little baby, I named her Karma for a reason. Everybody knows Karma means fate or destiny. Nobody has time to wait for fate to come back around and hell we might not even be around to see it when it does. Sometimes you just want to see the shit happen with your own eyes. My baby won't wait, she will help it along.

Karma will create her own fate, and the fate of those who choose to cross her. It is a choice, and Karma is a Bitch. They will see.

———— ⸺ ————

Karma was a smart little girl. She did good all through grammar school. We didn't have too many incidents. All except for the one time the teacher tried to get smart and snap off on my baby. This bitch, Ms. Davis picked the wrong Monday to try to call Karma out. Karma told me she was sitting at her desk doing her time tables. We both knew Ms. Davis was a stuck up bitch, but we put up with her just to get out of the fifth grade. Ms. Davis was sitting at her desk like she always did. I'm surprised her butt wasn't flat because that's all she did was sit there all day. She had a big ass mirror on her desk. She decided, I guess, that it was time to freshen up her lipstick. When Karma told me I thought, "What the hell she need to fix her damn lipstick for when she should be teaching? She better not still be fucking around with Mr. Andrews, the principal. Anyway, Karma said she was doing her time tables when her best friend Janeese whispered to her to ask about a 12 time table. She said 12 X 8, I think. Just as Janeese turned around Ms. Davis yelled, "Karma, shut it up." Karma said, "...but Ms. Davis...I...I." "I nothing, come up here and write on the blackboard, I will not talk five hundred times," Ms. Davis said. The class broke out in laughter. They started pointing at Karma and falling on the floor. Ms Davis said, "Now, Karma! You will not continue to disrespect my class young lady." Karma got up and started walking to the blackboard. She was rolling her eyes as she walked. She picked up the chalk, but the anger grew as she started to write...

I WILL NOT TALK
I WILL NOT TALK
I WILL NOT TALK

The kids were still snickering and Karma was getting heated, but she knew if she dropped a tear Ms. Gwen would whip her ass. Karma was writing and getting angrier by the minute. She started scratching the board she was writing so hard. She wasn't just pissed because she had to write this. She was pissed because she was messing up her new French manicure. In Karma's book, Ms. Davis just crossed the line. She continued to write...

I WILL NOT TALK
I WILL NOT TALK
I WILL NOT TALK

KARMA

She turned and looked at Ms. Davis who was now reading an Essence magazine. Karma just shook her head and wrote,

I WILL NOT TALK ABOUT MS. DAVIS DOIN THE PRINCIPAL IN THE GYM THE OTHER DAY WHEN I WALKED IN. MS. DAVIS BETTER NOT DISRESPECT THE GYM NO MORE! EVERYBODY TELL YO MAMA TONIGHT!

The class exploded in laughter. Some were saying, "Ooo, I'm tell...ing." Ms. Davis looked up from her Essence magazine and was holding her mouth open. She ran to the board and tried to erase it. It was too late. The damage had already been done. The entire class was in an uproar. Ms. Davis lost control of the classroom. At that moment, Janeese stood up and said, "Ms. Davis, Oh Ms. Davis, excuse me, Ms. Davis, did that say you was doing Principal

Andrews in the gym the other day? You so nas-teeee! I'm gon tell Ms. Gwen." Ms. Davis rolled her eyes at Janeese and started pulling her shirt down nervously. "Janeese, you and your little friend get your things. You are going to the principal's office," said Ms. Davis. Karma looked at Ms. Davis and smiled, she said, "Yes Ms. Davis, and by the way, my name is KARMA." Janeese was always the silly one. She got her bag and said, as loud as she could, "Are you comin with us to see the principal?" The entire class started falling out of their seats. Ms. Davis said, "I am calling your mother." Karma smiled to herself and said, "That will be on you. Call her. I ain't scared." Ms. Davis rolled her eyes and pushed them out the classroom door.

The girls sat in Principal Andrews' office waiting for Ms. Gwen to get there. Just as Ms. Gwen walked in the office Mr. Andrews walked out. Ms. Gwen said, "What happened here today?"

As Karma and Janeese started to explain to Ms. Gwen what Ms. Davis did, Mr. Andrews took her in his office and shut the door. They could hear them talking, and then it got loud and then it got quiet again. Karma thought she saw Ms. Gwen on her knees. She was wondering why she would be praying since it was Ms. Davis who started this whole thing. Maybe she was praying to get rid of her.

It seemed like the girls were waiting for at least forty minutes. They both walked out of the office smiling and Ms. Gwen said, "Ladies you get the rest of the day off. Come with me. We are going to get some lunch. Mr. Andrews said, "Good day ladies, see you tomorrow. Sorry for this misunderstanding." Ms. Gwen took us to lunch and for new French manicures. We were wondering why she was so happy and where she got all this money from. Anyway, we were happy about it. Ms. Davis should not have messed with us.

When we returned to school on Tuesday morning we had a substitute teacher. We heard someone say Ms. Davis wouldn't be back because so many mama's had called to complain about what happened in the gym. Karma graduated grammar school with no further incident and Ms. Gwen maintained her weekly parent meetings with Principal Andrews.

In spite of her temper, Karma was very smart. She just needed to stay focused. She was in high school now and she was in her last year. Ms. Gwen was so proud of her and she wanted her to go to college. Nobody in the Anderson history had ever gone to college, let alone finished high school. Ms. Gwen wanted that for her baby. She was gonna stay on her to make sure she got in a good college, and made somethin out of herself. She would never have to put up with anybody's bullshit. Now that's power! That's the power that Ms. Gwen wanted Karma to have.

2

KARMA & JANEESE

"What the hell do you mean you saw him with another chick? Who was the bitch?" Karma asked her best friend Janeese. Janeese just looked at her and said, "Girl just another piece of ass. You know that dude better than anybody. "

She was talking about Todd. Todd Jefferies. Karma and Todd had been dealing with each other for the last two years of high school. She had lost her virginity to Todd and he held a special place in her heart. Karma knew that she would love Todd forever. Todd was always there when she needed him. He was there when she cried about not having a daddy in her life. Todd told her, "It's okay, you don't need him. It's his loss. He is missing out on seeing what a beautiful daughter he has." That touched Karma's heart and she would do anything for Todd. She also knew that Todd liked to have sex and after she got in the swing of it, she had started liking it too but not as much as Todd. They both agreed that she would not get pregnant because they knew they were too young to get married and raise a family. Karma definitely did not want to have a child without a father in the home. She saw all that Ms. Gwen went through just trying to raise her with no help. She saw some of the things that Ms. Gwen had to do just to get by. Karma and Todd were in love and everybody at the school knew that they were an item. Todd had a wondering eye and hands too. He didn't want to get Karma pregnant so he spent some of his time with other girls.

Karma turned to Janeese again and said, "What the hell do you mean you saw

Todd with another chick?" "You heard
me," said Janeese. "Don't you mean
which one this time? You are a sucker
for Todd, and no matter what he does
you will still be letting him get up in
your face. So, why does it even matter
today?"

Janeese expressed her frustration with
the situation. She thought to herself,
"Karma has been putting up with
Todd's shit for so long, way too long if
you ask me. I don't know why she let
him get away with so much. She never
let anyone else get away with anything.
I guess if you hit the spot right all bets
are off."

"Karma, you caught Todd with that
skank Janet last year." Todd and Janet
were at the show sitting in the back row
getting freaky. Everybody knew what
they were doing. "

Candy Ain't Always Sweet**   **Page 25**

KARMA

"All I know", said Janeese, "is that they were all hugged up in the back row and he had his jacket covering them both, if you know what I mean."

So anyway, me and Karma walked in that bitch doing our Naomi Campbell walk, like we do. We had our popcorn and nachos with extra hot peppers. So, we walking... we walking, we doing our thang. All the guys in the theatre was gawking at us and wishing for just a few minutes alone with us. I opened the door to the theatre and what the fuck did I see? It was, none other, than Todd Jeffries' weak ass sitting there with Janet. I thought to myself, "Damn, Karma is gonna fuck them up fo sho." I started taking off my earrings. I was ready to throw down. I just held the door open and told Karma, "You go first Diva." I knew she would see that punk as soon as she walked in. Karma walked in the door and stopped. She looked right and she looked left, then she looked right again. I think she smelled his ass. Karma just started screaming, "Hold the fuck up! I know this ain't what the fuck I think it is."People started turning around to see what the commotion was. Karma said, "Wait a minute, turn the damn light on." She grabbed the usher and took his flashlight out of his hand. She turned the light onto Todd and Janet like they were in an interrogation room. Todd raised his hand to cover his eyes because he couldn't see. Karma said, "Todd Alphonso Jeffries, I know this ain't you. What the hell is under that jacket with you? Let me see what kinda trash the cat drug up in here." Janet peeked from under Todd's jacket. Karma bent down and got real close in Janet's face. She said to Janet in a voice that no one had ever heard, "Look Lil Bitch, get yo shit and get up and out of here before I make you wish you were dead."

Janet jumped up so quick, she slipped right past Karma. Janeese stuck her foot out and tripped her. She was just looking out for her girl. She said, "I have to admit it was funny as hell watching Janet lying on that dirty floor with her pants unzipped." She poured her large bag of popcorn with extra butter all over her head. Popcorn ain't cheap but Janesse felt that this was worth it.

Karma was still standing there looking at her sorry ass man, Todd. She was holding the nachos with extra cheese and extra hot peppers in her hand while she dealt with Todd. Todd started smiling nervously and said, "Baby, we wasn't doing nothin. She asked me to come to the show with her. She paid for it. I just wanted to see the movie." Karma stopped him, "Oh you just wanted to see the movie? Was the movie in her unzipped pants?" Todd said, "No, that wasn't what happened...see..." Karma held her hand up and said, "Don't talk Todd with your lying ass. I am sick of your lying and cheating. You got one more time and you are going to lose the best thing that ever happened to you. I will fuck your best friend on my way out." Todd stood up and said, "Karma baby, don't say that. You know what we have is real." Karma said, "Sit down Todd you wanted to see the movie. It looks like its starting." She pushed him back in his seat and said, "…and have some nachos." She dumped the nachos with extra cheese all over his shirt and started to walk away. She turned back and said, "Oh snap, I forgot you like hot peppers, extra hot peppers." She took the lid off of the peppers and threw it right in his eyes. He started screaming and said, "Karma you are wrong for that. I wasn't, oh my eyes are burning, get me some water." Karma said, "If I see that bitch Janet on the way out I will tell her to bring you some water and some popcorn." Janeese started laughing and said, "With extra butter."

Janeese shook her head and said, "Karma you went easy on him. You better be glad Ms. Gwen ain't around to see this. She taught you how to deal with these situations." Karma said, "I know, I know but its Todd, I love him." Janeese said, "Yeah okay, are we gonna watch the movie?" "Naw," said Karma let's get outta here before Ms. Gwen catch my ass slippin."

Karma has been my girl since grade school. Our families go way back. So, I know firsthand how crazy she can be. I couldn't believe she let Todd off that easy with just some hot pepper juice in his eyes. I have seen her do more for less. She definitely has a soft spot for him. She will be right back with him next week.

KARMA

Getting back to Todd, I introduced Todd and Karma about two years ago, one day at the bowling alley. Karma didn't really seem to like him at first. She told me he was okay, but he didn't really float her boat. She said she could take him or leave him. She didn't see anything special about him. I know he stayed up under her the whole night like she was a dog in heat. I don't know what happened after that, but they have been an item ever since. I know they talked a lot and became really close friends.

Karma was my girl. We grew up in the same projects. My mama and her mama were best friends. When my mama died, Ms. Gwen took me in like one of her own. Me and Karma have been sisters ever since. When I breathed in she exhaled. We were real tight and everybody knew not to mess with us. Everybody knows Karma is a bitch and Karma would do anything to protect her family. I was her family. Me and

Karma were like twins only we didn't look alike. We were both fine though, ask anybody. They will tell you. We were always known for dating only athletes and guys who had cash. We didn't care where they got it from, as long as they were willing to spend it on us. Our hair was always laid, feet and nails always on point. Yes, we were divas and designer label hoes. We trusted each other with our lives. I had her back and she had mine. If anything ever happened, we both went down for it. We were excited because it was our last year in high school and we both wanted to go to college. Nobody in either of our families had ever gone to college and we were determined to break that mold. Plus, Ms. Gwen wasn't trying to hear anything different. She had already said she had a man waiting on us to leave so he could move in. I think I saw principal Andrews from grammar school sneaking out of the apartment one morning. Ms. Gwen likes to keep it real.

So, we were under pressure to get out of her house anyway. It was our last semester, and we were on target to get the hell out of high school. We were anxious to be grown and get out there and see some stuff. We had secretly been drinking and hanging in clubs all year. This summer we were planning to do some stripping to earn some money for college but we had to get past this last semester without any trouble.

Sure as shit, we had a problem. Karma told me she was called to Mr. Samuel's office. Mr. Samuel's was the Algebra teacher. He was real slimy, everybody knew that about him. He didn't look bad or dress bad. He just always seemed to be walking up behind you when you weren't looking. ...Just slimy. I heard last year from Karla Kennedy that she had to sleep with Mr. Samuel's

to get an "A" in his class. She said he
approached her with the option of
taking the "F" in algebra or to give him
some cookie for an "A". Karla said she
thought long and hard about it but she
was headed to college and she did what
she had to do. She got the "A", so I
guess it wasn't all bad. Karla said he
was good and she slept with him one
more time for the road before she left for
school. He paid her too. ...Old slimy
freak ass. Well I was hoping Karma's
meeting went okay and we didn't have
to do nothing like that. I had to wait
until Karma got home to find out what
happened.

In the meantime, Karma went to Mr.
Samuel's office. She knocked on the
door and Mr. Samuel's called out, "One
minute." She stood there waiting. A
few minutes later, Janet Winters walked
out.

She was a junior and she was the same skank that I had caught with Todd on a couple different occasions. As she walked out, I looked her up and down and said, "hmmmph, I bet I know what you was doing skank." Janet looked at me but decided not to say anything. She was right because I was waiting to punch her right in her goofy ass mouth. She walked away.

Mr. Samuel's came to the door and said, "Ms. Anderson, come in I've been waiting to speak with you." I walked in and he seemed a little close as he shut the door. He said, "Please take a seat." He had some kinda classical music playing on his IPod. I had never heard that shit before, but he was just smiling and hummin along. I sat down. I said "Mr. Samuel's, you ain't got no Drake or Nikki Minaj in that IPod? What is you listening to?" He sat down and started rustling his papers. He looked over his glasses at me and smiled, he said, "Ms.

Anderson, did you mean, what ARE you listening to?" I just looked away and said, "Yeah, what you just said. " He looked at me this time as if he was looking through me, he said, "I am listening to a Sonata in G for Violin and Piano, Nice isn't it? "

I ignored that stupid ass question. He was looking down at his papers and talking to me at the same time.

He said, "Ms. Anderson you need to expose yourself to different things. You know, you don't know what you like until you give it a try. I know you are planning to go to college. You need ex po sure young lady." He looked up and smiled. I just cleared my throat and said, "Um, Mr. Samuel's I have a note that says I needed to come to your office. That's why I am here." I was thinking to myself, "Why don't you expose me the hell to why I am here." Mr. Samuel's sat his stack of papers down and looked at me and said, "Ms.

Anderson you are here because you are a last semester senior who needs to get at least a "C" in my class to graduate and at the present moment, my love you have an "F" in my class. And I will assume that you are representing Janeese Block as well. You are the spokesperson, correct? Ms. Block is running an astonishing, "F" as well. So, what are we to do?" "I don't know Mr. Samuel's. "What can we do? We have to pass your class, because we have to graduate and we have to get in college. Why would you wait until now to tell us? We only have a few weeks left. Can we do some extra credit?" Karma pleaded. Mr. Samuel's sat there listening and humming his classical sonata or whatever the hell he said it was. He looked up at the ceiling and said, "Hmmm, extra credit. How much extra credit would one need to do to come up from an "F" in just a few weeks? Let me see…" He tapped his fingers on the desk. I was getting nervous, I was starting to sweat and I knew I couldn't cry. Ms. Gwen would beat my ass if she ever heard about it. I gotta get through this. "Mr. Samuel's, there has to be something that I can do. I cannot **NOT** graduate and Janeese can't either. That is not an option." said Karma. Mr. Samuel's stood up and said, "Not an option? Oh, I see and I totally understand your position Ms. Anderson." He started walking toward me and went behind the chair that I was sitting in. I had my head down, I was distraught and was trying to hold back my tears. Mr. Samuel's ran his finger along the side of my neck. I jumped because it scared me. He said, "Don't be worried Ms. Anderson. I am certain that we will come to an agreeable solution to this little problem. I know how important it is for you to graduate. I went to college and it is an experience that I would hate for you to miss." He lifted my head and looked in my eyes, "We will work it out." He said. "Are you hot Ms. Anderson?

There appears to be a trickle of sweat running down your shirt." At that point he took his hand and caught the sweat before it ran between my breasts. He tapped my thigh and went back to his seat. I was thinking, "Damn this trick is trying to get in my pants. All I'm trying to do is go to college. What about Todd?" I exhaled. Mr. Samuel's looked at me and said, "I think I know of an extra credit opportunity...away from here. Do you know what I mean?" I said, "No Mr. Samuel's I don't think I know what you mean."He looked me straight in the eye and said, "Karma don't come in here playing this Ms. Goody Two Shoes act with me. If you want the grade you will have to produce." Produce what Mr. Samuel's? I said. He leaned into me and whispered, "I have seen your tight ass and Janeese at the strip club performing. I liked your pole routine and I would like you to perform that for me...in private." said Mr. Samuel's." "What grade would we get if we do it?" I asked.

He said, you will both receive a "C" that would be enough to get you through but I just want you, not Janeese. You represent her, correct?" "Yes, Mr. Samuel's" I said. He reached across the desk and touched my nipple. He started twirling his freaky finger around, he said ..."and I want a lap dance since there are two grades involved." I thought about it for a minute and said, "I want an "A". I knew I had him he was a getting excited sitting there. He surely thinks with his dick. That was his first mistake because I control the dick, and judging by the tips I had been getting at the club, I am doing okay in that area....but not algebra. Mr. Samuel's said, "Deal" with a big ol' slimy grin on his face. I would swear I saw some juice trickling down the side of his mouth. I just shook my head and thought "eeww how weak. " I got up to walk out and slimy said, "Oh...Ms. Anderson, I do have some Nikki Minaj and Drake at the house. I will see you soon."

I almost lost my lunch and walked out of his office. I headed home to break the news to Janeese...Damn, what about Todd?" I was walking and thinking... and thinking and walking.... I was thinking it won't be so bad. After all, we had been dancing at the club for a couple months now on the down low. They hadn't let us do any lap dances yet, but I knew I could do it. I wanted that "A". I would make sure Janeese got a "B" too. He tryna play us cheap with a "C". Mr. Samuel's is a punk, but I am going to get what we need and probably some cash too. He can't handle the truth.

I started thinking about Todd again. I know I love me some Todd Jeffries. He just had that effect on me. I just felt so close to Todd, he was my BFF, after Janeese of course. I trusted Janeese before Todd. After all Todd had a roving eye, hands and dick.

I know Todd would lose his mind if he knew I gave Dave Samuel's a lap dance, Oh Lord! But Todd wasn't thinking about me when he was with Janet. Fuck him! I have to get mine. I went home to tell Janeese the plan.

3

LEON'S CLUB

It was hot as shit when I walked in the house. I think Ms. Gwen was frying some chicken. Lord knows Ms. Gwen could lay it down and I was shole hungry after that meeting. I walked in and yelled, "Janeese, Janeese where you at girl?" Janeese was in the kitchen with Ms. Gwen waiting on that chicken to drop.

I walked in the kitchen and said, "Hey Ms. Gwen. Hey, Janeese wassup?" Ms. Gwen looked at me and put her hand on her hip and said, "Wassup is you better bring your narrow ass over here and show Ms. Gwen some love girl." I laughed and walked over by the stove. I gave Ms. Gwen a hug and she hugged me real tight. I said, "It is hot as hell up in here. That's gonna be some good ass chicken." Ms. Gwen smiled and said, "Yeah, y'all gonna have to eat and go. I got a smoking hot date tonight and I don't need no spectators!" We just looked at each other and said on cue, "Ms. Gwen tryna get it in." We laughed and said, "Okay Ms. Gwen."

Ms. Gwen never cared if we cuss or talk to her like we all the same age. She raised us that way. She likes to keep it real and that worked for us. If anything ever went down, Ms. Gwen would kill somebody about us. But we both know she taught us to handle our own business.

Janeese looked at me as if to ask with her eyes, "Wassup with Samuels." I said quickly before Ms. Gwen could catch on, "Girl we can go hang out after we throw down on this chicken and give Ms. Gwen some free time. "Janeese smiled and said, "Kool."

Me and Janeese had to find something to do. We had to stay gone for several hours so we decided to go to the club and make some change. On the way to the club I filled her in on what had happened at the school. Janeese said, "Damn, he is a low life. I guess the only way he can get some ass is to give out some grades. Karla Kennedy told me she had to sleep with that fool too so she could graduate. She said he wasn't bad and she did him one more time for the road and he gave her some money to spend at college." Karma looked at Janeese and said, "I ain't sleepin with that trick. He said he wanted me to dance and that is all I am going to do. He better not try to touch me. If he tries any funny business I will get our grades, graduate and then report him to the authorities. He really don't want none of me or Ms. Gwen." Janeese shook her head as we walked in the club.

I heard the DJ playing R. Kelly's, "Twelve Play" as we went to get dressed. We were both hoping we got some good songs tonight so we can make some money. The music has a lot to do with our performances.

We went to get dressed and had a drink before going on stage. Ms. Gwen always drank Jack Daniels and that's all she kept in the house. Me and Janeese started drinking Jack and Coke. That's what we were drinking before our turn to dance came around. I was coming up next and I had a buzz.

I got my cue and I went out to Eric Benet's, "Chocolate Legs." I loved that song. It was so sexy. I was ready to set it off in there and make some money. I threw down. There was so many tips coming my way, I had to figure out how to get them all. If they have a strip club at college we won't ever have to worry about money. I was on stage shaking

KARMA

my ass. I went to the edge of the stage and started twirling it. The men started yelling and screaming like they had never seen anything like it. Some started coming up to the stage and sticking tips in my thong. I turned around to look. It was so dark in there that you couldn't really see anybody's face. There was a man walking toward me. He had what looked like a twenty dollar bill in his hand. He stuck it in my thong as I gyrated. I smiled and mouthed "Thanks boo". He came back and stuck a piece of paper in my thigh highs. I smiled and prepared to leave the stage. My time was up. The manager, Leon had to come out with a bucket to get all of my tips. I was so excited. I heard him saying, "Look like you boys like Ms. Mocha Latte. She will be back".

That's what they called me. They couldn't use our names because we were under age. Janeese was going on next. When I got in the back, I had another Jack and Coke to bring me down. I started pulling all of the money out of my ass crack and I remembered the paper that the man left in my thigh high. I pulled it out and opened it. It said, *"See you and Nikki Minaj next week. I can't wait. D."* I stopped counting my money for a minute. I couldn't believe that he came here tonight. Man, he is so slimy. Imma have to get some more money from his slimy ass to put in our college fund. I focused again on counting my stash. $1,000; $1,200, damn I got $1,560 for dancing for twenty minutes. Do I really need to go to college? Just kidding… Ms. Gwen would whip my ass and hang me out to dry. We are going to college in August and we will have a nice stash when we go. I hope Janeese comes out okay, she's good but she ain't as nasty as me, I thought to myself. I will have to work on her. Janeese cleared $800. That's more money for our fund.

It was late. Ms. Gwen's company should be gone. We went home and passed out. "Next week I gotta deal with D, damn," thought Karma.

4

MR. SAMUEL'S

We only had one week left until our graduation and we were starting to get a little nervous. Ms. Gwen was telling everybody in the world that her babies were graduating and going to college. She had the world on high alert. You would have thought there was some kinda terrorist event expected to occur. All we had to do was to make it happen. That meant I needed to get with Mr. Samuel's before the grades were posted. I would stop by his office today. I was cleaning out my locker and throwing everything away when someone walked up behind me and covered my eyes. I knew it was a dude because he was so close up behind me I could feel him bulging and breathing down my neck. I said, "Stop playing, I am a grown ass woman and I ain't got time for no kiddie tricks. I am graduating next week." I turned around to see Todd's fine ass standing there. My heart dropped to my feet. He always had that effect on me. My heart started beating fast but I caught myself. I had been playing Todd to the left ever since the last time I caught his ass messing around on me. I love him, but…" Todd said, "Oh you a grown ass woman now? Are you too grown for your man? Todd put his arm around my neck and said, "Can you walk with me? I want to talk to you." I wanted to talk to Todd but I couldn't. I knew I had to go see Mr. Samuel's. I said, "Naw baby, not good for me." Todd's eyes looked sad. I was wondering what he wanted to talk about. He just looked at me and said, "I need to see you real soon. Will you call me?" I said, "Okay" and walked away.

I waited until Todd was gone and the coast was clear.

I went to Mr. Samuel's office. I knocked
on his door because he definitely had a
closed door policy. He was standing by
the door and when he opened it, out
walked Amy Stewart. I think she was a
sophomore. "He is getting her ready
early," I thought to myself. He said,
"Come in Ms. Anderson, I have been
expecting you." Amy ran off real quick.
I walked in, but before I could take a
seat or say a word he closed the door
and pressed me up against it. He started
breathing heavily as he leaned into me.
He said, "Hellooo, Ms. Mocha Latte, I
have been waiting to see you after the
other night. Damn, you know how to
work a pole, don't you?" I said, "It's
just dancing on the side to get money
for college." He grabbed me and pulled
me close. He whispered in my ear, "I
put a $100 bill in that red thong that you
had on and there is a lot more where
that came from." I pulled away just as
he was sticking his tongue in my ear.
"Mr. Samuel's I need to get our grades
entered," I said.

"I need an "A" and Janeese needs a "B". He said, "No worries baby I already entered them. You are going to graduate. Now you owe me a little something. Here is my address, he handed her a piece of paper, what time can you be there tonight?" "I will be there at eight," I said. He smiled and said," I will be waiting...and bring that red thong with you." I walked away and he was just grinning and watching me walk. I was thinking to myself, "This will be like taking candy from a baby. This dude is sprung. I am going to work him over tonight and get some more money for the college fund." I felt good about it.

Now, I need to catch up with Todd. I called Todd's cell phone. No answer, so I headed home. I called again and it went straight to voicemail. I was thinking he must be messing around with that damn Janet again. My calls never go unanswered. I called him back and left a message:

Hello Todd, This is Karma. Remember me? At one time I had your heart but it seems those days are long gone. You and Janet look real good together. I am a grown ass woman and I ain't dealing with this simple shit no more. Don't worry, be happy. Goodbye Todd Jeffries.

I hung up. I was walking home thinking about me and Todd and getting angrier as each moment passed. I was so mad at Todd. What we had was supposed to be special. I guess he wanted to tell me that he had moved on with Janet when I saw him in school. He did look really sad when I saw him. Anyway, I tried to get up with him and he didn't answer, so fuck him! Ms. Gwen ain't raise no fool. It's time for me to deal with some grown woman shit. I'm about to go to college.

I was so mad at Todd for the rest of the evening. I had told him all of my innermost thoughts and secrets. He knew me better than anyone. I told him about Charlie, the father that I had never seen. Nobody knew about Charlie except Janeese but she doesn't know how I really feel about it. He broke my heart, but I ain't no punk bitch and I ain't gonna cry about it. Ms. Gwen would not have that anyway.

Just then Ms. Gwen yelled from her room..."Karma, Todd has been stalking you all day, why don't you call that boy back? "I just said, "Okay Ms. Gwen," but I knew I wasn't calling him back. I wasn't gonna waste any more time loving somebody who didn't love me back and I wasn't turning my head anymore. Todd will get what's coming to him. Let him keep fucking with Janet.

I was so pissed thinking about what happened with me and Todd. I had to have a Jack and Coke to ease my nerves. Ms. Gwen had some Honey Jack this time, so I tried it. It was good. I made a great big glass with ice and Coke and went to my room to prepare for the night.

I started getting my dance outfit ready and the red thong. He was going to pay to see this red thong. Shit, he had already put the grades in. I didn't even have to go, but Hell I didn't trust his slimy ass. I started getting dressed. I was looking hot, as usual. I had on a yellow Aeropostale polo shirt with the cute little butterfly on it and some skin tight Apple Bottom jeans. Now that Todd had betrayed me, this apple was ripe for picking. I was thinking, "It's time for me to leave the boys alone. I am graduating and I need a real man in my life." I wondered what one would look like. I think the Jack and Coke was talking more than I was. Anyway, I put on my bright yellow, three inch, high heeled pumps. As I looked in the mirror, I asked myself, "Who could resist all of this? I mean, they do have eyes. Don't they?" I left the house. As I was walking you could see every crease and crevice in those jeans. I headed to his house and I was thinking this won't be so bad.

I rang the bell and the door opened immediately, as if he was standing there waiting. He said, "Hello Ms. Mocha Latte, you look very nice today." I smiled and said, "Thanks Mr. Samuel's." He said, "Please call me Dave." I said, "Okay". I walked in and he offered me a drink. He was drinking gin and all I knew about gin was what I had heard Ms. Gwen say many times, "Gin make you sin." I said, "Do you have any Jack and Coke?" I wasn't tryna do no kinda sinnin so I stuck with what I knew. He brought my drink. I took a sip and said, "Where is your bathroom?" "He grabbed me by the hand and escorted me to the bathroom. His hand was warm and soft. It reminded me of Todd. I thought to myself I better slow down on this Jack and Coke. That almost felt like Todd.

He said, "Can I watch?" I said "No, I want you to be surprised. You wait in there okay" He started smiling and said, "Okay." When I came out he was sitting in this big chair like he was waiting to watch TV. I guess gin does make you sin because he had taken his pants off and was sitting there in his boxer shorts. I walked out wearing a skimpy, red laced negligee that hit right below my butt cheeks. The top had a bustier style with a push up bra in it. The girls were sitting up saying "Hello".

Of course, I had on the red thong that he had requested. I had some five inch, red, come fuck me pumps that drive the men wild at the club. I had oiled my body real good before I came out so I was looking real slippery. Men like that. As I walked around to the living room I noticed that he had a stripper pole. "Mr. Samuel's really is a freak." I thought to myself. "Who really has a stripper pole in their living room?" I was in shock! When I turned around he was standing right behind me. He started trying to grab me and rub on me. I said, "Dave, slow down baby. I think we need to establish some ground rules before we go any further." He licked the side of my neck and sat back down, wide eyed. If I'm not mistaken, Dave started rubbing himself. I started talking, "Okay, you will get a pole dance and a lap dance. You can look all you want but, you cannot touch, is that understood?" As I turned around to look at him I noticed a large stack of twenties and hundreds. It had to be a thousand dollars, easy. I didn't want him to see me looking at the money. So, I walked over to him and bent down and said, "Davey do we have an understanding sweetie?" He started licking his lips and touching my breast. I mean they were sitting up there saying, "Touch me." So, I stood back up and said, "Dave let's get some music going." Dave was still drinking his gin and he got up and walked to the IPod. I went by his pole and got ready to do some tricks for him. I was waiting to see what was going to play. He walked over and kissed me. I pretended that he was Todd for a minute because I wasn't leaving without that cash. He stuck his tongue in my mouth and slid a twenty in the bustier. I thought, "Okay." It was starting out good, but I needed him to put more money in quicker so I would not be here all night. Either way, I knew the money was leaving with me. So, I turned around and bent down, real slow and touched my toes. He liked that. I felt him slide several bills in my thong as he started rubbing my ass. I knew then that the ground rules were out the door, but I wanted all of that money. I wiggled up from the floor like a snake. I slowly stood up and the music started to play. It was Maxwell, "Pretty Wings." I went over to the pole and jumped on. Dave sat on the floor right in front of me. He didn't want to miss anything. It was okay with me because he had the tips and I wanted them. I started sliding up and down the pole.

I climbed up to the top and flipped upside down and held my position in a Chinese split. Dave jumped up so quick he almost scared me. While I was in my split, he slid a couple of hundreds in the front and started rubbing them around in my coochie hair, while he tried to get a feel. He walked around behind me. I had mad abs, so I could hold that split for as long as I wanted. He pulled up my negligee and ran his tongue across the string of my thong. I heard him moaning and I was thinking, "Put the money in Dave." He slid a bill across my ass crack like it was a credit card machine. He walked back to his spot on the floor. All of this money and attention was making me hot. I had a bucket the size of an ice bucket on the floor. I came off the pole and put my tips in. I always kept a bucket with me. Ever since that day at the club when I couldn't get all of my tips up off the stage. We took a drink break. I stepped off to the kitchen to get my drink and Dave had his gin. That Jack was working on me. I was feeling real loose right now, like I only wanted to feel with Todd. "Todd who?" I asked myself. I shook it off and ran my hand across Dave's face. I said, "Davey, do you have some music ready for the lap dance?" He took his hand out of his lap and grabbed the remote. I could see that he was real excited. I had never seen a man pole quite as large or as hard as his. I wasn't sure what to do as far as the lap dance went. I didn't want to sit on his slimy dick. I heard him cue the music. It was Eric Benet, "Chocolate Legs" again. Dave said "This is our song. I fell in love with you that night at the club Ms. Mocha Latte." I started my dance. I did a few gyrations in front of his chair. He leaned back and exhaled as if he had died and gone to heaven. I did my dance real slow on the front and then on the back. He was rubbing my legs. I walked up closer to his chair. I put my right leg on the arm rail and winded it up for him real slow. I was trying to avoid that slimy dick. I did the same thing with my left leg on the chair. He loved it! I straddled him in the chair but he had this huge obstruction so I couldn't really sit on his lap. I gyrated just above him and he kept trying to pull me down. He grabbed me and sat me in his lap. I started thinking about Todd as I felt the heat from him between my legs. He took a big stack of bills and put them in my bustier. I started feeling very hot. I eyeballed the stack of bills, it was going down. "Just a little more cash and I am outta here," I thought to myself. Just then Dave grabbed the insides of my thighs and picked me up. He laid me down on the floor and started licking all over my body. I do mean all over my body. I was so dizzy from the Jack that I didn't even try to stop him. I remember hearing Tre Songz singing, "Neighbors Know My Name." I remember him screaming out, "Mo...cha...La...tte," Mo...cha...La.. .tte," real loud. I must have fallen asleep. I felt something wet between my legs. I didn't know if I had dropped some ice from my glass or what. The room started spinning. I just wanted it to stop. I tried to sit up and I saw Dave's head between my legs. The room started spinning again, so I lay back down and that is all that I remember. When I woke up Dave was lying next to me. He was sleep and holding his crusty dick in his hand. I didn't know what happened! Jack Daniels had never done that to me before. Damn, I was slipping. Ms. Gwen would beat my ass about some shit like this. Somehow, I lost control of the situation...But When? And what actually happened?" I started playing it back in my head. I got up slowly, I was still kinda woozy and I felt really sore between my legs, and wet. When I got up to go to his bathroom to get dressed, I saw some vibrators and fake penises lying on the floor. I got my clothes so I could get the hell outta there. I tiptoed past Dave and the empty gin bottle that was on the floor. I grabbed my bucket and the rest of the stack and got the hell up outta there. I didn't even try to wash up before leaving. I needed to get out. I went home feeling sick.

I got home and everybody was asleep. I took a shower and got in the bed. What the hell happened to me? The next morning Janeese was shaking me saying, "Karma, Karma what the hell happened to you last night? Did you go? What took so long? What happened?" I told her about the night and she said, "It sounds like he put something in your drink." I was sick to my stomach. I ran to the bathroom and vomited, repeatedly. I didn't want Ms. Gwen to hear me. Janeese stood outside the bathroom door with a cup of green tea saying, "Drink this you will feel better. By the way, Todd got tired of calling for you and he came over here last night and waited for about an hour.

"Damn, I really screwed up last night. I don't know what happened to me. I like dancing but I love the money more. We had another thousand to add to our college fund. But Lord, please let me be okay. Why am I so sore down there? I don't know if I will ever have the answers. I will have to fake it until I can make it, because I have to find out what's going on with Todd.

Todd was at home wondering what was going on with Karma. He was hoping that she hadn't forgotten about him, because he still loved her and had hopes that they would still be together. Todd was going away to college also but none of them knew where they were going yet. No matter what happened he didn't want to lose Karma. He really did love her. Janet was just a distraction and an easy lay for him. She wasn't even good in the bed. She was just something to do because he didn't want to get Karma pregnant. They had a pact. So, now he was wondering where Karma had been so late last night and why she hadn't returned his calls and why she left that message about being a grown ass woman and stuff. Todd was wondering if he had lost his soulmate. He knew she had been preoccupied with something at night lately. He assumed it was another guy. He didn't know that she had been working in the club. She barely spoken to him since the last incident with Janet. Anyway, tomorrow was graduation day and he would try to talk to her then.

5

GRADUATION

At six am Ms. Gwen was up and wide awake! She was making breakfast and had the coffeepot going. She was just singing, "Today is graduation day. My girls are going to college." She repeated the same tune for a good thirty minutes. Who could sleep, with all of that racket going on? Karma and Janeese were very excited about graduating from high school. Karma was still feeling a little woozy and just a little sore down below. She decided not to say anything about what happened and suck it up.

"Dave Samuel's will get what's coming to him," she thought.

Ms. Gwen was in the kitchen on the phone. "Yes Girl, my babies are graduating today, Yeah they both goin to college too. No honey! Now you know you can't break them two up." Ms. Gwen went on and on. One call after the next. She was so excited, and of course her man would be moving in at the end of the summer. We started getting ready and listened as she made the next call. "Hey Poochie, Wassup Baby. Yeah my babies are grad-u-ating to-day, she said, and of course they are going to college. I wouldn't have it no other way. Now you know Ms. Gwen don't raise no fools' honey. Oh they are both smart"….she went on and on.

Karma and Janeese looked at each other smiling…Karma said, "Te –le -phone". Janeese said, "Te –le -gram," They both said in unison, "Tell Ms. Gwen," and they both rolled over laughing. They got dressed and headed off to the graduation. Ms. Gwen had a big celebration planned after the ceremony and she had invited at least five hundred people. She was so excited and she had been cooking cakes and pies and everything else all week.

When we made it to the school, we put on our caps and gowns and took our seats. Me and Janeese were right next to each other and Todd was in the row behind us. We waited for all of the speakers to finish and for them to call our names. We were so over high school. Just then, we heard Karma Anderson.....Ms. Gwen went crazy! I thought for sure she was going to have a heart attack or get put out of the ceremony. As I walked across the stage and waved at Ms. Gwen, I noticed a strange man standing next to her. He was real dark skinned. I had never seen him before. He was smiling real hard. All I could see was his teeth and his eyes. I wondered what secret Ms. Gwen had been keeping. Then I heard.... Janeese Block... Ms. Gwen went into phase two of her stroke...That's my baby too. Would y'all look at my baby walkin across that stage? They going to college too," she screamed at the top of her lungs. Then we heard Katie Brown, John Harrison... and all of the other names in between until we heard, Todd Jeffries...Oh Lord, please help Ms. Gwen. "That's my baby too y'all. I am so proud of all of my babies today," she said. As Todd walked across the stage I felt a little pain in my heart. I decided I would try to talk to him after the ceremony and invite him back to the celebration.

In the meantime, I was still wondering who that man was with Ms. Gwen. I know she had her different men. I had never seen this one before and she seemed so excited. She actually invited him to my graduation. I was scratching my head on that one. We had our diplomas and our grades. I noticed that slimy David Samuel's sitting on the stage. I pulled out my grade report to see my "A" and wouldn't you know it, slimy gave me a "C". I thought, "That's kool. I got something for his slimy ass."

We told Ms. Gwen we would meet her at the celebration. I wanted to take care of something and catch up with Todd. I told Janeese what happened with Mr. Samuel's. Fortunately, Janeese had her purse and she always had a sweet tooth. I said, "What you got in that purse Janeese?" She said, "I got some Reese's Pieces and a couple Twix bars". I said, "Give me the Twix." Janeese said, "Can you use the Reese's Pieces? You know how I feel about my Twix. I looked at her like, "are you serious?" I yelled, "If you don't give me those damn Twix, I'm about to beat you down right here in this parking lot. We can get you some more." She handed it over but held the end of it for a minute. I told her, "Come on we got work to do." We walked toward the parking lot and looked for Mr. Samuel's beat up hoopty. "There it is," Janeese said. I said. "Okay, you watch my back." I leaned up against slimy's car and peeled the gas tank open. I knew his slimy ass wouldn't have a lock on his gas cap. I opened the Twix bars and politely dropped in three whole Twix, and another for good measure. I grabbed the Reese's Pieces and poured the entire bag in the tank. I closed the tank and tapped it twice. In a couple days, Mr. Samuel's would learn that candy ain't always sweet.

We laughed and went to look for Todd. We walked back around by the building and I saw Janet standing there. I stopped. I wanted to see just what was going down. We waited and low and behold who walks up to her, but Todd Jeffries in the flesh. Todd stood a distance from her. It looked like they were arguing. I saw Todd waving with his hands and talking loud. He seemed like he was pissed off at whatever she was saying to him. All of a sudden, she grabbed him and started hugging him. I said to Janeese, "Well ain't this the little happy family." Then Todd pushed her off of him and she started crying. She sat down on the ground with her head in her hands sobbing. Todd walked away.

Now I really wanted to know what was going on with this situation. I skipped right past Miss Janet and tried to catch up with Todd. I was running now, in my heels, calling, "Todd, Todd, hey, I know you've been trying to reach me. What's up?" Todd said, "What's up with you? I been blowing you up." I said, "I know, I just been trying to get my ducks in a row so I could get out of here." Todd said, "You been playing me real shady lately. I thought we was tight." I said, "Yeah I thought that too, but judging by your little girlfriend over there, I'm no longer in the picture."

"No, that's not true. You know my heart belongs to you," Todd said. I looked at him and cut my eyes, I said, "but obviously your dick belongs to Janet." I turned to walk back toward Janeese and he grabbed me and wouldn't let go. He said, "Karma, don't do this. I need you, we need each other." I said, "Did you think about that when you got with her? I turned and pointed toward Janet. He said, "She is buggin. She means nothing to me. I want to see you today." I invited him to come to the celebration that Ms. Gwen had planned. He said, "I will be there." He left and so did I.

I walked back past Janet who was still sitting on the ground crying. I turned toward her and said, "Sucker". Janeese screamed out in laughter. I had to get to

the celebration and see who that man
was with Ms. Gwen.

—— ⟩⟩⟩⟩ ——

We went back to the house and changed
into some jeans and tanks with high
heeled sandals. We wanted to be
comfortable, because we knew Ms.
Gwen was gonna drag this out for as
long as she could.

I was hungry and anxious to hear what
was going on with Todd. He wasn't
there yet, so I got my plate. Ms. Gwen
had laid it out. We had ham, fried
chicken, fried catfish, roast beef and
string beans with macaroni and cheese,
candy sweets, potato salad and cole
slaw. Ms. Gwen prepared everything
herself. She wouldn't have it any other
way. She made a 7up pound cake,

KARMA

caramel cake for Janeese and a peach cobbler that would make you smack your momma. I heard Ms. Gwen across the room, talking saying, "Yeah baby, you know Ms. Gwen throws down. I ain't no punk in the kitchen. Now try some of that peach cobbler."

I needed to know who the man was. I was preparing to go over and introduce myself, just as Todd walked in the door. My heart skipped a beat. I started feeling some kinda way when he walked in the room. Todd was like family. He had been around so long everybody knew him and liked him, but they didn't know about Janet. Only me and Janeese knew about that. Todd was walking toward me when Ms. Gwen said, "Todd, baby come on over here and get some of Ms. Gwen's cooking baby. You look like you need a good meal." Todd said, "Yes, Ms. Gwen, I sure do. " He walked toward her. I was watching his every move. He had on a white polo shirt and you could see how muscular he was when he wore that shirt. Ever since he played on the football team he had been into pumping iron. He had the guns and the six-pack to prove it. I wish I could just grab him and hold him and tell him what happened with Mr. Samuel's, but I ain't stupid. That would never happen. His Levi's was hitting him just right. He looked good enough to eat, standing by all that food. I started to tell him to get on the table, but I remembered he was messing around with Janet. I would wait to hear what he had to say about why she was crying earlier. I sat down and watched him eat. I didn't see the man that was with Ms. Gwen anywhere. I would have to ask her later who he was. When Todd finished eating we decided to slip away and go back to the house and talk while no one was there. I told Janeese we were leaving but she was so wrapped up with her new guy, Carlos. I don't think she heard a word that I said. So, we just left. Todd was holding my hand as we left the community center. I knew Ms. Gwen would be there until they closed it down. She had to talk to everyone there at least twice about her girls. There were at least five hundred people there, not counting the kids. So, me and Todd would have some time alone to hash things out.

It felt like old times walking with Todd holding hands. My heart was aching because I felt that he had messed everything up between us. We got in and I offered him a drink. He didn't want anything. We went to my room and sat down. He said, "Come here Karma, sit next to me. So much time had passed since we were alone or had time to connect like we used to." I said, "Well I would hate to be the one to bring it up, but there is a certain problem that we have named Janet." "Karma, don't be sarcastic I am serious and I am here to let you know how much I love and care about you and no one else," he said. I said, "I appreciate that, but your actions have not shown that. How could you love me so much and be doin what you do with Janet?" Todd wrapped his arms around me and looked me right in the eyes and said, "Janet is nothin to me. You know she was just sex and only that one time. We had a pact and I didn't want to get you pregnant before we were able to get married. I started tricking off with Janet and I couldn't get rid of her. That girl is psycho. She knew up front about the two of us. I told her that we were in love and no matter what happened it would always be Todd and Karma." "Well if she knew all of that why was she crying at the graduation today?" I asked. Todd hesitated. He said, "Karma, I love you baby. You are the only person for me," and he started kissing me. He said, "I want to make love to you and show you with my heart what you mean to me." He took off his shirt and I forgot my name. He stood up and took his pants off and I couldn't say one word. He took my clothes off, one piece at a time. He leaned over and kissed me again and a single tear fell from his eye into mine. My heart started burning and he got under the covers with me. Todd was different than he had ever been before. He was passionate and so serious at that particular moment. I forgot all about Janet. He touched every inch of my body with his finger as he talked. "Karma you are the future Mrs. Jeffries. I think you know that. We have a bond that no one can break. I mean no one. You are me and I am you. We are one. We will always be together, no matter what." I closed my eyes. He began to kiss me gently all over my face and neck. It felt like my body was rising off of the bed as Todd performed his magic on me. He entered me so gently but still strong. We locked into each other. It felt like one person, rising and falling and moving around from left to right; right to left. Todd wasn't rushing like he usually did. This time we both began to cry and our tears were intermingled. It really felt like we were one as he had told me. He whispered as he looked into my eyes, "I love you Karma."

It was magical and I had never experienced anything like it before. My mind was so messed up with everything that had happened in the last couple of weeks, but this felt right. This was the only thing that felt right. Perfect! I was excited about me and Todd getting back together and he was too. Before he left he was happy again and smiling but he still seemed a little different, but I believed him. Todd was very serious when he was talking to Karma as he gave her one last hug and said, "Can I see you tomorrow?" She said, "Yes." Karma felt he had been very forthcoming and honest about what happened with Janet.

What Karma didn't know was that Janet was pregnant. Todd couldn't bring himself to tell her that. He left quietly and went home. Todd had a lot weighing on his mind as he got home. He knew he didn't want to lose Karma and definitely not for Janet. He had to figure out a way to make this all work out and make Janet go away. "Damn, I really screwed things up this time," he thought to himself. Todd looked in his bedroom mirror and said, "It's not going down this way. I am not going to let that bitch Janet bring me down. I will think of something before Karma finds out about this. "I love that girl." Janet is such a skank. She has been with lots of boys. "How do I even know this baby is mine?"

Karma was up talking to Janeese. It was Saturday, and it was official. They were free from high school and they considered themselves grown ass women now. Karma said to Janeese, "We need to start hitting the club at least three nights a week now since we are out of school. We gotta keep our stash tight. We don't know what college we goin to yet but we gotta have our money right." Janeese said, "Yeah, you right. We ain't tryna be no broke asses in college." They agreed that they would kick it off tonight. Janeese asked Karma, "What happened with Todd last night?" Karma explained to Janeese what she and Todd had talked about. Karma told Janeese that Janet didn't mean anything to Todd and that Todd loved only her. Janeese said, "Well, why was that trick Janet crying at the graduation? "Karma pondered that question and said, "I guess because he told her he didn't want nothin else to do with her trifling ass.

Anyway, the way we were last night was magical. I could tell that he didn't want nobody but me. We love each other and when it's all said and done we will be together."

Janeese rolled her eyes in her head and said, "Yeah okay Mrs. Jeffries. By the way, you owe me two Twix and a bag of Reese's Pieces and I want them today." They both laughed.

Karma got serious for a minute and said to Janeese, " Jay, did you see that dark dude that was at the graduation and the celebration with Ms. Gwen?" Janeese said, "Yeah, I peeped that. I was wondering who the mystery man was. He must not be from around here, but Ms. Gwen shole was cheesing." "I know, right" said Karma, "I ain't never seen Ms. Gwen sweat no man like that. I mean, she get down for hers but she ain't usually doing the sweatin. You feel me?" Janeese said, "Yeah, you got that right. Ms. Gwen ain't no punk bitch. Maybe we just need to ask her who dude was. Maybe that is who she got moving in when we move out." "I don't know but as soon as she gets up, I am all over that", said Karma. "Me too", Janeese added.

"Now can we get some breakfast? I'm hungry," said Janeese. "Yeah, you always hungry. What else is new? You better lay off of the snacks if you gonna make top dollar at the club like me," said Karma. "I do alright", said Janeese, I ain't been getting no complaints. "Carlos don't count," said Karma, "Just remember the college fund."

They went to eat breakfast at the local dine-in spot. "That's where you get the best breakfast," Janeese would say. Ms. Gwen was still asleep and Janeese wanted some pancakes with strawberries and whipped cream. Karma started eating her omelet and immediately felt sick. She ran to the bathroom. Janeese started to go check on her but she wasn't leaving those pancakes for nobody. Karma came back to the table looking like a ghost. Janeese said, "Damn, did somebody beat you up in there?"Karma said, "No, but it's something wrong with this food. They tryna poison me up in here." Janeese continued to eat her pancakes and said, "Well it shole ain't nothing wrong with these pancakes." Karma shook her head and said, "Let's go, I need to talk to Ms. Gwen."

6

CHARLIE AIN'T MY DADDY!

They hurried back to the house to talk to Ms. Gwen about the mystery man. When they got to the house, Ms. Gwen was in the kitchen humming some tune. "Hi Ms. Gwen," they say in unison. "Oh hey babies, where y'all been?" she asked. We went to get some breakfast, said Janeese as she rubbed her belly. Karma started, "Ms. Gwen, at the graduation yesterday...before she could finish her sentence Ms. Gwen interrupted. Baay bee, everything was so nice. It was all so beautiful. I am so proud of my girls and y'all going to college too. Thank you Lord! My heart is so full right now, she said. Karma waited for a pause and tried again,

"Well at the celebration there was a...."Yes baby I know, the celebration was nice too and did you try that peach cobbler? I really stepped all up in that pie, didn't I Janeese?" Janeese was about to concur when Karma stood up and said,

"MS. GWEN, STOP IT DAMMIT! WHO WAS THAT MAN WITH YOU?"

Ms. Gwen turned around and looked at Karma and said, "Hold up sweetie. Don't get too damn grown for your own damn good now. You know Ms. Gwen will slap the damn taste out of your mouth." Karma said, "But Ms. Gwen, I am just tryna find out who that man was, I never saw him before." Ms. Gwen said, "Okay but act your age baby. Sit down right here and we can talk about it." Janeese and Karma sat at the kitchen table anxious to find out who the man was. Ms. Gwen sat down and said, "Baby girl, that man was Charlie."

"CHARLIE?" Karma yelled and stood up. "YOU MEAN CHARLIE, MY SPERM DONOR CHARLIE?"

Gwen said, "Sit down chile and calm yourself. Act like you got some damn sense in this house." Karma was getting really angry with Ms. Gwen. This was serious business and Karma felt like Ms. Gwen was being too casual about it. Ms. Gwen said, "Karma, yes it was your daddy Charlie."

"WELL WHAT THE HELL DID HE COME FOR? HE AIN'T EVEN SAY ONE WORD TO ME! DO HE THINK HE JUST GONNA SHOW UP AFTER ALL THESE YEARS AND BE THE PROUD FATHER?

NO! NO! NO! IT AIN'T GOIN DOWN LIKE THAT! WHERE WAS HE WHEN I NEEDED HIS BLACK ASS? WHY HE COME NOW SHINING HIS EYES AND TEETH? ARE YOU SLEEPING WITH THIS FOOL? YO ASS IS SLIPPIN MS. GWEN!!!!!!"

Ms. Gwen stood up slowly, moved toward Karma and slapped her so hard she almost fell down. Janeese just sat there amazed at what had just happened. She knew it was best for her to stay out of it.

Karma ran to her room and slammed the door. She laid in her bed thinking, "How could Ms. Gwen betray me like this? This dude has never been a part of my life. He has never come to see me or sent me a penny. Now he just supposed to show up and we gonna be a big happy family? I don't think so!

KARMA

Ms. Gwen can kiss my ass. I don't need her or Charlie." She fell asleep; she was feeling really tired. Karma slept for hours. She would still be sleeping if it wasn't for Janeese waking her up.

Janeese shook and shook, "Karma, wake up…" "What Janeese?" Karma asked, as she wiped her mouth with her hand. Todd is on the phone. He has called at least ten times. Can you pleeeease get up and talk to him?" Janeese said. Karma rubbed her eyes and said, "Oh okay, here I come." Karma struggled to get out of bed. Her entire body was sore and she felt nauseous.

She got up and made her way to the phone, "Hi Todd", Karma said. Todd said, "I thought you said I could see you today." "Okay, she said, "Just come over here, Janeese is going out with Carlos and Ms. Gwen is going to the prison to see Tyrone. She won't be back for a while." Todd said, "Okay I will see you in about an hour." "Okay", she said. Karma went to take a shower hoping that it would make her feel better before Todd arrived.

7

T-BONE

Ms. Gwen waited patiently for the prison bus to arrive. She knew she would be on the bus for a while. She had borrowed Janeese's IPod and some magazines. She had one of those National Enquirer papers. Ms. Gwen liked reading about celebrities and their problems. For the life of her, she could not understand why the people who had everything didn't know what to do with it.

This would be her last bus ride to go and visit Tyrone. He would be getting out in a couple of weeks. Tyrone Jonathan Andrews, Jr., Tyrone was Ms. Gwen's first baby. He came five years before Karma. She should've known Tyrone would be trouble when she first laid eyes on his daddy.

Tyrone's daddy is how Ms. Gwen earned her PhD in Bullshitology. If there was ever some shit going on, Tyrone was behind it. Tyrone was one of those "Lying Libras". Whenever he opened his mouth, out popped a lie. He couldn't even control it. It took eight years for Ms. Gwen to figure it out, but by that time it was too late. She had already birthed the liar's son. As if that wasn't enough, to add insult to injury she let him convince her to name his son after him. It was eight years of one lie after another. Tyrone lied so good, he even believed it. Ms. Gwen started believing it too.

Like the time Tyrone was missing for a whole week. Ms. Gwen didn't know if the fool was dead or alive and no one else had seen or heard from him either.

Ms. Gwen had given him up for dead, but sure as shit, he showed up on Sunday in time for dinner. He came to the back door smiling and smelling good with a box of pixies and a dozen long stemmed yellow tea roses. Tyrone knew Ms. Gwen had a weakness for chocolate and she loved her yellow tea roses. He said, "Hey Gwennie, I missed you baby." Ms. Gwen said, "Hi Hell! Where the hell you been?" Come on in here and give me my chocolate. Now, where the hell you been?" Tyrone started smiling and scratching his forehead as if he was Detective Columbo. He moved closer and started rubbing on Ms. Gwen. She opened the box of chocolate and popped one in her mouth and said, "So where you been Ty?" Tyrone looked her straight in the eye as he continued to rub his forehead and said, "Uhhh, baby you ain't gonna believe this but, me and my buddy Paul got a one week job out of town. We just did some odd jobs all week and you know I didn't think about nothing but you. So here I am with your chocolate and roses baby. I just got back. " Ms. Gwen knew it was another one of his lies. She didn't feel like arguing with him. She accepted his story and went back to the chicken she was frying. Tyrone took off his shoes and sat in the recliner in front of the TV for the rest of the night. As far as he was concerned, He was back in.

It took a while, but Ms. Gwen found out that Tyrone was married and was living a double life. The damage was done. She had his son.

Ms. Gwen was relaxing and eating some of the snacks that she borrowed from Janeese's private stock. She was happy to be making this last trip. She had mixed emotions about Tyrone's release. She was glad her son was getting out but she hoped he was ready to get his life together. Even though he was her son, she hoped that he had a place to stay. Ms. Gwen did not want Tyrone back with her. Now that Karma and Janeese were going away to college, she had plans for her own happiness. Tyrone went to jail for armed robbery. Ms. Gwen did the best that she could with Tyrone but she knew he had too much of his daddy in him.

Tyrone and some of his friends came up with a scheme. They wanted to get enough money for all three of them to get some gym shoes. It was some kind of Air Jordan shoes that cost almost $200 a pair. They decided to rob the corner store in the neighborhood to get the money. I don't know why they would rob a store in their own neighborhood. They knew everybody in and around the store knew them by name. I don't know where Tyrone got the gun or the balls to go into that mans store and stick it up. Before he got in there good, the police pulled up to go in and get some donuts.

Ms. Gwen, shook her head and thought to herself, "My Chile, My chile, he ain't got the sense that God gave a bessie bug." He ain't got no common sense. Tyrone got seven years and he will be getting out in about a week on probation. He had good behavior while he was locked up. Go figure," thought Ms. Gwen.

The bus pulled in to the prison lot. Ms. Gwen started collecting her things. As she prepared to enter the prison, the guard pulled her to the side to check her out. The guard was a young man who looked like he could've been a body builder in his spare time. Ms. Gwen started smiling and said, "Who me?" She stepped to the side and he ran the wand up and down her body. He asked her to turn around, she said, "Baby you look like a good ol' piece of candy, medium chocolate....with caramel...oo baby and nuts too." She grinned. He blushed and said, "Thank you maam."

Ms. Gwen told him, "You better be careful with those hands before Ms. Gwen take you in one of these rooms and show you how to get down..."Cougar Style." She smiled and winked at him as she walked through the gate. She was still talking as she walked through the gate, to no one in particular she said, "yall got all these fine ass young men up in here rubbing on Ms. Gwen. One of em gonna mess around and catch me on payday and get Alllll my money and baybee bye, That's it that's all." All of the security staff started laughing and said, "Hey Ms. Gwen."

She proceeded to the table to wait for Tyrone to come out. As soon as he entered the room, Ms. Gwen stood up and said, " Hey Baby, T-Bone, Ms. Gwen is over here sugar." Everybody looked her way. Tyrone wasn't embarassed by her. Everybody knew Ms. Gwen and loved her.

She kept it real. Some of the inmates in the visitors room waved at Ms. Gwen. Tyrone sat down at the table. He said, "Hey Ms. Gwen, you lookin good today." Ms. Gwen said, "How the Hell did you think Ms. Gwen would be lookin boy? You ain't never seen me lookin no other kinda way." She said, "You look like you could use some mustards and turnips and some of Ms. Gwen's good ol fried chicken. Ms. Gwen gonna cook you something when you get out. Tyrone said, "I'm getting out next week. Can you get my daddy to come pick me up?" Ms. Gwen said, " I will call his triflin ass but I will make sure somebody come get you T-Bone. Ms. Gwen ain't never let you down." They continued their visit.

Todd showed up in exactly an hour from the time he called. Karma had finished her shower and gotten dressed. She felt a little better than she did earlier. She was still very upset about what happened with Ms. Gwen earlier and the fact that Charlie decided to show up. Todd and Karma sat down at the table to talk. They both had sad eyes. Todd started first, "Karma, what is wrong with you? You look like you lost your best friend and I am right here. I told you we would always be together no matter what." Are you doubting me?" Karma looked at Todd and started crying. She told him about what happened with Charlie coming back. She said, "It hurt me so bad that he had the audacity to come here and not even say a word to me and Ms. Gwen acts like everything is okay." Todd said, "Don't cry Karma. Don't worry about that. You've made it all this time without him and you will be okay. I'm sure Ms. Gwen has an explanation for all of this. She has always had your back." I know, said Karma, She just caught me off guard with all of this.

What was it that you wanted to talk to me about?" Todd looked like he was about to cry. Karma said "What's wrong Todd? Why are you looking that way? Is this about Janet?" Todd straightened up and said, "No Karma, Janet is nothing. I am sad, but it has nothing to do with Janet. The reason I am sad is because my parents are sending me away for the summer to earn money for college. I have to leave tomorrow." "Oh my God, Are you serious right now?" We just got back together. What am I supposed to do all summer without you? This can't be happening. First it was Janet, then Charlie, and now this? My life is falling apart and it should be the happiest time of my life," Karma said and started crying again and went to her room to lie down. Todd followed her and stayed there for as long as he could. Shortly after their talk, Todd got up and started for the door. He assured Karma that he would text and email. He didn't have the heart to tell her the truth about Janet. Karma dozed off thinking about her day. Janeese came home and reminded Karma that it was Saturday and that they were working at the club that night. Karma was so upset that she just started packing her bag. She didn't say a word to Janeese about what happened with Todd. She would just tell her later.

8

MS. MOCHA LATTE

Ms. Gwen made it back from the prison late that night. The girls had already left for the club. Ms. Gwen was glad to be at home alone. She needed some time to unwind and prepare to deal with Karma and the Charlie situation. Before Ms. Gwen went to bed she laid the envelope on Karma's bed that Charlie had left for her. That night at the club Karma was feeling a little off. She just did not feel like her normal self. She chalked it up to everything that had happened in the last couple of days. She shook it off and told the bartender, "Jack and Coke, easy rocks. She took her drink and went in the back to prepare for her performance. Karma was on her second drink when she heard the MC say, "Fellas, get ready for your favorite and mine, MS. MOCHA LATTE and she is on fire tonight. Have your money ready!"

She heard the DJ cue the music and it was a Jamie Foxx song called, "Unpredictable". Karma said to herself, that's perfect. I'm feeling a little unpredictable tonight anyway. Let me go out here and get this money. She stepped on the stage and the crowd went crazy.

Karma worked the stage with confidence like she owned it. The men made their way to the stage bringing their tips. Some already knew the routine and put it in the bucket. Others wanted a chance to touch her so they brought them to her or her thong. She didn't care, as long as they brought them. She saw hundreds, twenties and some of the cheaper guys brought tens.

Karma didn't care. It all added up. As she moved to the front of the stage, she bent down and opened and closed her legs slowly. The crowd roared. She saw someone walking toward her. It was slimy Mr. Samuel's. He pulled out a twenty and rubbed it between her breasts. She took the twenty and stood up. Karma thought to herself, he must be having engine trouble and smiled.

As she stood up, she decided to bend back over and pull her thigh high up. When Karma turned around there stood a beautiful specimen of a man. He was so fine Karma might have given him a private dance. He had on a business suit and as he walked to the stage he loosened his tie and made eye contact with Karma and smiled. He touched her leg and then stuck a card in her fishnets. No money, just a card. He returned to his seat and she started wrapping up her routine. She picked up her bucket and went to the back. She could hear the men screaming for an encore. Leon never allowed encore performances. He wanted them all to come back again. Karma got another drink and changed her clothes. She waited for Janeese to finish so they could leave. She started counting her money while she waited. "Damn, $2000 tonight and one business card." She wondered what that was about. She thought, "Surely this dude don't think I am going to call him. Yes, he was a sweet caramel looking guy and fine as all hell, but I ain't calling him. That's just not going to happen. She looked at the business card. It read:

Michael T. Buchanan, Esq.
Attorney At Law
Buchanan and Associates
1 (800) 332- 5567
www.miketbuch@banda.com

"Hmmm, what could he possibly want?" she wondered. She put it in the envelope with the cash and forgot about it. Janeese was up next and Karma was glad because she was really tired.

When the girls got home, they were both exhausted and Ms. Gwen was asleep. They went straight to their room. Karma noticed an envelope on her bed. She was too tired to deal with it tonight. She laid it on the floor and would deal with it tomorrow.

In the morning, Ms. Gwen was up and at it early. She was in the kitchen fixing breakfast and singing, "What a Friend We Have In Jesus". Karma was thinking to herself, Ms. Gwen musta got some last night. She know her ass ain't religious and she ain't been **NO** friend to Jesus. Karma was still angry with Ms. Gwen. Karma snapped out of her train of thought and remembered the envelope on the floor. She picked it up and it smelled like Dolce and Gabbana, *Light Blue for Men*. Karma loved that scent. Todd wore it when he wanted to impress her. She read the writing on the front. It read, *"Baby Girl"*. She held it for a minute with mixed emotions and decided to open it. Karma slid her finger through the back of the envelope to break it open. Inside there was a letter. When she unfolded the letter a check fell out. The check was made out to: **Karma Marie Anderson;** the amount was **$5,000.** The note section read, **My Baby Girl;** signed, **Charlie Washington.**

Karma sat on the bed and stared at the check for a good fifteen minutes as if she was in a trance. Janeese woke up and said, "Karma, what are you doing?" Karma showed her the check. Janeese's eyes bulged, almost out of the sockets. She jumped off the bed and proceeded to do the touchdown dance that football players do when they score. She said, "College Fund." Karma looked at her with sadness in her eyes. She handed the check to Janeese to put in the college fund box. Karma thought to herself, "That is one check that I will never cash." Karma went to the bathroom and turned the shower on. She closed the lid of the toilet and sat down. She opened the letter.

Karma,

Baby, this is real hard for me as I know it is hard for you. I know it is not right for me to show up now that you are a grown woman, and a beautiful young woman you have become I might add. This is hard for me because I know I am wrong but sometimes it's hard for a man to accept a sudden situation such as having a baby unexpectedly. Don't get me wrong, I was in love with Ms, Gwen and we had a truly beautiful relationship that we started, but everything happened so fast. I just didn't know how to handle it and honestly I was scared to deal with it. I was just unsure of what to do. I know this doesn't make you feel any better but I'm just trying to explain myself. Baby believe me my heart has bled a little each day that I didn't spend with you. You are my blood.

Karma started crying. Her tears dropped heavily right on to the letter. She wiped them away and continued reading.

I feel like I am less of a man for walking out on you. It has been so hard to face you. I have maintained contact with Ms. Gwen and I have pictures for every stage of your life. I have treasured the pictures all of these years and I have hated myself for not being there to raise my daughter. I woke up. I know I overslept but I don't want to spend another day without being a part of your life.

I know you are headed off to college and I want to be there for you. I also know the little money that I have been sending Ms. Gwen over the years will never make up for the quality time that we should have spent together.

Baby, I am sorry but let's start now. I have enclosed a check for $5,000 for you to use as you see fit for college.
I will pray that you will call me or write me before you leave so we can get this relationship started.

Oh, by the way, you have a sister who just graduated high school also. Her name is **Anjinique.** She will be going to college too. I would like for the two of you to meet.

Love
Daddy!

Karma didn't know what to think or say, or do. She was truly overwhelmed with everything that had happened. Karma started feeling faint and felt a sudden wave of nausea hit her. She got hot all of a sudden and her mouth started watering. She jumped up off the toilet and opened the lid just in time to spill her guts. Karma kneeled to the floor and prayed to the porcelain Gods. She was whispering, "Lord, please just take me, this is all too much." But in the back of her mind she heard the voice of Ms. Gwen saying, "Karma, get your ass up. Now you know you ain't no punk bitch. Put your big girl panties on and shake a leg. Ms. Gwen ain't raised no fool." Karma sat there for a few minutes then got up and took her shower. When she exited the bathroom, she felt all eyes on her. Janeese and Ms. Gwen were waiting for her to come out. They both knew she had taken the letter in there with her and they were anxious to hear what Charlie had to say. Janeese had already told Ms. Gwen about the

$5,000 check. Ms. Gwen was smiling, she thought it would be a good thing for Karma to have her father as a part of her life. Janeese didn't pull any punches, she said, "So where's the letter?" Karma just looked at them both and shook her head. She tossed the tear stained letter on the table and went to her room to finish dressing. Karma put her clothes on, and lay back in the bed. Before she knew it she was fast asleep.

In the kitchen, Janeese and Ms. Gwen read the letter and both sat there crying.

Ms. Gwen had a lot to do today because T-Bone was coming home and she needed to change the sheets on the let-out couch. Ms. Gwen thought to herself, "That boy ain't got nowhere to stay and dammit to hell, he was coming back home." She gathered up everything that needed to be washed, but she wasn't a happy camper. Janeese went to her room to check on Karma and saw that she was sleeping again. She decided to go and spend some time with Carlos. She stood there for a minute wondering what was really going on with Karma. They had to dance at the club tonight, so she just let Karma sleep.

Karma woke up after a few hours and just laid in her bed thinking about the letter from Charlie. "Daddy", she thought. "How the hell does this dude deserve to use that title with me? ...the money that he has sent to Ms. Gwen? That hussy ain't never told me about no money. Ms. Gwen is shady...and I got a damn sister, the same age as me. What kinda shit is that? **Anjinique**, that sounds real boojie to me. I bet she didn't have to wonder who her daddy was. They all got this shit twisted and I don't need his damn guilt money. I am doing fine all by myself. To hell with all of them, Charlie, Todd and Ms. Gwen.

I am working the club tonight. I'm good," thought Karma.

KARMA

9

I KISSED A GIRL

That night at the club, Karma ordered
her usual, she wasn't ready to
experiment with anything new yet.
"Jack and Coke on the rocks please", she
said and can you put it in a tall glass?
And go easy on the Coke too, she
added.   Karma was angry and she
needed to unwind before her
performance. She thought to herself,
forget all of them. I can meet some new
people. Besides, the people here at the
club definitely love me. While Karma
and Janeese were in the back getting
dressed, Leon, the manager approached
them and said, "Look here, we gon try
something a little different tonight."
They looked at each other and then back

at Leon and said, "Yeah okay, what?"
He had a sneaky look on his face and
moved in closer because he didn't want
the other girls to hear him. The girls
were already angry because Karma had
been getting all the tips and when they
came out to dance the tips were few.
Leon smirked and said real slow, "Look
here, I want you two on the stage; he
paused for a minute and quickly said,
"together". He held his hands up in the
air as if he had caught a stroke of genius
from the most high. He said, "The men
will lose their freakin' minds and Imma
introduce y'all as Salt and Peppa, so get
ready. Leon was so excited. He left the
room.

The girls looked at each other surprised,
but thought about the college fund and
agreed it would be a snap. Janeese said,
"It's like taking candy from a baby."
Karma said, "Bet". Karma and Janeese
had danced around in their room
together for years, they were sisters after

all. They drank up while they waited for the music to cue. They heard the music begin to play, it was a song that they didn't recognize but they knew that a true dancer could dance to any music or none at all. Karma went right and Janeese went left. They each worked their side of the room. The men were screaming and pulling their wallets out. Suddenly, the song said, *"I kissed a girl and I liked it"*. They made eye contact and started moving toward center stage. Karma went down in her signature Chinese split and Janeese did a side split. The money bucket was running over. Leon slid out and put another bucket on the stage. When they stood up, the song said, *"I kissed a girl and I liked it"*. Karma reached over and grabbed Janeese behind her head and bent her down and kissed her right in the mouth with her tongue. Janeese was in shock but played along. The men lost it. They were standing on the tables. One even yelled, "Please pick me", as he stood there with his hand up like he was in class. Karma let Janeese go and then kissed her finger and touched her butt with it as if she was putting the fire out. They left the stage.

Security had to come and subdue some of the men. The girls went to the back to change and decided to wait and count the money later. They both went to the bar to get a drink and since they were instant celebrities, men were sending drinks from around the room. As they stood at the bar to get the first drink, someone walked up close behind them and whispered in Karma's ear, but loud enough for Janeese to hear, "You never know what's in your drink, ha ha." They both turned around and it was none other than slimy Mr. Samuel's. Janeese said, "And you never know what's in your gas tank either", before she knew it. Karma just rolled her eyes at Janeese. Karma turned around and said to Mr. Samuel's, "Let me find out that you fucked with my drink and that's your ass. You will regret it for a long time." He smiled and said, "That's not all we did...I have some more cash. When are you coming back? It was realll good." Karma threw her drink in his face and Janeese had to hold her back. Security came and escorted him out. Karma told Janeese, "He is going to pay!" Janeese asked Karma, "What happened that night?" Karma said, "I don't really know." They got their things and left the club.

When they got home they sat down to count the money. They ended up with $3,500 and one business card. Karma didn't even notice Michael there. She was so into the routine. They added the money to the college fund box. Karma had that look in her eye and whenever she had that particular look, nothing good would come from it. Janeese saw Karma's face and remembered Ms. Davis from fifth grade.

They were about to call it a night when Ms. Gwen stuck her head in the door and said, "Hey babies, y'all been kinda scarce round here. Don't get caught up, cause y'all goin to college." Janeese said, "Okay Ms. Gwen." Karma put her head under the cover. She knew Ms. Gwen always knew when something was up and she didn't want her to see her face. Ms. Gwen added, "Y'all know T-Bone will be here in a day or so, so we need to get some groceries in here. Y'all know that boy can eat." Janeese said, "Yes Ms. Gwen."

Ms. Gwen walked away and went back to her room. She picked up the phone to call T-Bone's daddy. She dialed the number for Tyrone's raggedy ass, so he could pick T-Bone up from the prison. Ms. Gwen dialed the number. Tyrone's wife answered as if she had snatched the phone right out of the wall, "HELLO!" She said angrily.

Before Ms. Gwen could get a word out, she said, "WHO THE HELL IS IT? And she yelled, "Tyrone come get this damn phone, it must be one of your skanks on the phone cause they ain't saying nothing." It sounded like she threw the phone. Ms. Gwen heard some rattling. Tyrone finally answered, "Uh, Hello", he said. "Tyrone, this is Gwendolyn Anderson. You really need to get that bitch in check before I have to come over there and do it for you! You feel me?" she said. Tyrone said, "Oh, Hi Ms. Gwen, what's up baby?" Ms. Gwen corrected him, "Don't baby me! Are you going to pick your son up from the prison tomorrow?" Tyrone said, "Uhh, I just talked to T-Bone. He know I'm gon get him." Gwen said, "Good! Bye," and hung up the phone. She didn't have time for Tyrone's Tom Foolery. She might mess around and catch a case herself messing around with him. She went to sleep.

The girls woke up and had to go to the grocery store to prepare for T-Bone's arrival. Karma really wasn't ready to deal with T-Bone. Sure she hadn't seen him in five years and yes he was her brother, but she remembered all of the problems he caused when he was there. She really wasn't looking forward to any of it. She knew how slick her brother could be. She needed to start hiding her things and find a safe place for the college fund. T-bone could not be trusted. Janeese on the other hand was excited about the return of T-Bone. T-Bone always had a crush on Janeese and she looked forward to the attention.

The next afternoon, Leon called and asked the girls to pick up an extra shift. He said a couple of the girls didn't show up. He wanted to know what time they could be there. Leon suspected some of the girls were leaving to go to a new club that was about to open.

He didn't want Karma and Janeese to leave. The two of them kept his crowd coming in and the larger the crowd the more drinks he sold. Leon made his money off of the door and the drinks. Karma agreed to do it. She was starting to think she needed to get as much money as possible. She was still very angry with Ms. Gwen and thought she might need to find a place for herself and Janeese before they left for school. She wasn't feeling easy about T-Bone coming home. She convinced Janeese to do it.

They got to the club and followed their normal routine. They ordered Jack and Coke, on the rocks. They prepared to perform again as Salt and Peppa. Karma wore a white bustier and thong. Janeese wore a matching set in black. They stood in the wings waiting for the DJ to cue the music. They knew this song right away and they were ready to do it. The song was Jamie Foxx, "Blame it on the Alcohol". They got on stage and did their thing. Janeese started to loosen up and added a few more tricks to her routine. Karma jumped on the pole like a spider. She climbed up as high as she could and turned upside down into her signature Chinese split move. She held it for a few minutes and slowly slid down the pole about an inch. She turned around and did the same move. She was still pretty high. Her plan was to inch down like a centipede and get all the tips she could get. All of sudden, Karma fell to the floor, head first because she was still upside down on the pole. Janeese heard the loud thud and ran to Karma. Karma was out cold. The DJ stopped the music. Janeese lost it, "Oh My God, Oh My God! Is she breathing?" Leon ran out to see what had happened. The men stood silent, waiting to see what was going on with their favorite girl. Leon announced, "She fainted. Everybody stand back. Can somebody call a damn ambulance!" Janeese was no help. She was running back and forth across the stage like a caged bird who wanted out. She was making Leon nervous. He looked at her and said, "Janeese, put your ass in that chair right there and here eat this Snickers."

Janeese sat on the opposite end of the stage shaking her leg and eating her Snickers, waiting for the ambulance to come. Some of the girls brought clothing for them both to put on. Karma was coming to. The crowd started clapping when they saw her sit up. They were both dressed by the time the ambulance came.

Leon insisted that they go to the hospital. At the hospital, Janeese was still a nervous wreck she didn't want to but she thought she had better call Ms. Gwen. Karma was still being examined. She dialed Ms. Gwen's number. The phone rang about five times when someone finally picked up, it was T-

Bone. He answered, "Anderson Residence" in his most professional tone. Janeese smiled for a second recognizing his voice she said, "AAH Hello?" He said, "Talk to me baby." Janeese said, "Hey T-Bone, What's up?" "T-Bone said, "Is this my baby Janni?" She smiled into the phone and said, 'Yeah, it's me!" T-Bone asked, "Where y'all at? I been waitin for you and Karma to get here." Janeese whispered into the phone as if Ms. Gwen was on her end, "T-Bone, we at the hospital. Karma fainted." He said, "SHE DID WHAT?" Janeese said, "Be quiet, please don't wake Ms. Gwen up. Can you come down here? I don't know what's wrong yet, she is still in the examination room." T-Bone said, I'm on my way," and hung up. When T-bone made it to the hospital, Janeese was sitting in the waiting area eating a bag of plain M&M's. He said, "Hey cutie pie, Where is Karma? Is she okay?" She replied, "They haven't told me anything yet." They sat down and caught up on what had been going on. Karma came from the exam area walking slowly and holding her head. T-bone jumped up, "What up sis? What's goin on wit you? He reached to hug her." Karma said, "LET'S GO!" The three of them walked out of the hospital and T-Bone had a million questions. Karma started crying. Janeese said, "Karma what's wrong? Tell us before we get back to the house. Karma broke down. She knew Ms. Gwen didn't allow any crying but she felt this situation called for it. She stopped walking and said, "I'm pregnant!" "You're what?" said Janeese? T-Bone said, "Damn, what y'all been getting into since I been gone?" Janeese hit him in the arm. Karma said, "I'm pregnant and I think..."you think what?" Janeese said. Karma cried and said, "I think... I think that bastard raped me! T-Bone said, "Wait holdup, what you talking about? What Bastard? Are you still with Todd?" T-Bone asked. "Somebody need to tell me what the hell is goin on, before I snap the fuck off."

Janeese looked at him thinking, "It sounds like you snappin the fuck off already to me."

Karma looked at Janeese and said, "You never know what's in your drink," Janeese looked back and they said in unison, "It was realll good". Janeese said, "Oh DAMN!" Karma said, "Oh DAMN is right. His ass is in trouble and Imma see that he pays for this." T-Bone said, louder this time, "Is somebody gonna tell me what's goin on?" Karma said, "T, Janeese can fill you in on everything that happened. We can't let Ms. Gwen find out. I gotta figure out how to get this demon out of me.

"They walked in the house. Ms. Gwen yelled from her room, "Where y'all been?" T-Bone said, "We was just catching up Ms. Gwen. We goin to bed now." He looked at Janeese and said, "You can sleep right here with me." She hit him in the arm.   He smiled. Karma went straight to bed. She was furious. She was so mad she couldn't even sleep. She lay awake thinking of how she would get Mr. Samuel's back for good. She saw a note that said Todd had called.

Janeese and T-Bone stayed up until the sun came out. Janeese filled him in on everything that had been going on.

When they finally woke up, they all were tired. They decided to take a day off. The three agreed to go to the show and grab a bite to eat afterwards. Karma decided that she should call Todd back. She dialed his number. There was no answer. She left a message.

KARMA

Hey, Todd. This is Karma. I was returning your call. T-Bone is back home and we are on our way to the show. You can call my cell phone if you like.

She hung up.

At the movie theatre, Janeese and Karma saw a lot of kids from their old high school. Karma went to the concession stand to order some popcorn. Of course Janeese wanted candy. As they stood in line, Karma happened to look to the right. Out of her periphery she was sure she saw that skank, Janet. She tapped Janeese on the arm and said, "Is that that skank, Janet over there?" Janeese said, "Yeah that looks like her, but she looks like she...Janeese caught herself. Karma said, "Yeah I know, she looks like she's pregnant! I'm going to ask her for myself."

Janeese followed while T-Bone placed his order. Karma walked up to Janet and pulled her away from the counter. Karma said, "What's up skank?" Janet didn't say anything. Karma said, "I said what's up skank? What you been up to?" Karma pushed her. Janet said, "Leave me alone, if you know what's good?" Karma couldn't believe her ears. She said, "Oh you got this twisted. You don't want to front right now. Are you getting fat?" Janet said, "Ask your man if I'm getting fat," and smiled. Karma said, "I'm asking you hoe; now you better talk." Janet said, "I think you need to talk to Todd. " She started walking away and she turned around and said, "Our baby is due in December, and rubbed her belly," she walked away. Karma wanted to kill Janet and even more than that, she wanted to kill Todd. He had betrayed her for the last time. Right at that moment, her cell phone rang, the name on the screen flashed, **Todd.** The movie was about to begin but Karma answered the phone anyway.

Hello? said Karma. Hey baby, it's me, Todd. How's it going? I miss you so much – You are my life Karma.

Karma rolled her eyes up in her head and thought, "If I am your life, then you are dead."

Karma said, "Yeah what else is going on?" He said, "Nothing, just working and thinking about my baby."

Karma thought, "Poor choice of words."

She said, "Well, I'm about to go into the movie now." Todd said, "I Love you! I will call you later."

Karma just hung up the phone. She gave him a chance to come clean. She vowed at that moment to never speak to Todd again.

Karma had so much on her plate; she couldn't even remember what movie they saw. She thought of everything that she had on her plate: Todd, Janet, Charlie, Ms. Gwen, Mr. Samuel's, being pregnant, college...and Michael was still a mystery. She felt her world was really closing in around her.

Leon from the club called early to check on Karma. He told her to take some time and get herself together and don't come back to work until she was better. Karma was pissed, she needed to keep working and keep the money coming in. She also needed to take care of her situation. She didn't tell Leon that she was pregnant. She just said, "Okay Leon" and hung up. Karma thought to herself, "Janeese was still able to perform so she would have to hold the college fund down by herself for a while."

Karma had a busy day ahead. She started by calling the clinic to make an appointment. She looked at her phone and noticed that Todd was calling. She hit the "Ignore" button. She looked at the phone and said, "Are you serious?"

Janeese was performing at the club alone that night. She invited T-Bone to come along and see her performance. She still had a secret crush on T-Bone. Karma told them to go on without her, she was just gonna stay home and try to figure some things out for now.

Karma took a shower and put her pajamas on. She went to the kitchen to get a cup of chamomile tea. In the kitchen, she ran into Ms. Gwen. Karma and Ms. Gwen hadn't really talked since the incident with Charlie. Ms. Gwen said, "Hey baby, you stayin' in tonight?" Karma said, "Yes." and started making her tea. She wasn't trying to be around Ms. Gwen because she would know something was wrong. Before she could get away, Ms. Gwen said, "Karma, sit down baby. I think we need to talk." Karma didn't want to, but she knew it wasn't a question, so she pulled up a chair and sat down. Ms. Gwen said, "We need to talk about Charlie and what is going on with you and Todd? That boy been calling my phone like he need it to breathe. So what's really going on? I know you are angry about Charlie..." Karma said, "And you're not?" Ms. Gwen said, "Baby I have learned that sometimes things don't work out like we want them to. Sometimes, we don't get to pick what's gonna happen, but we have to deal with it and try to make the best of a bad situation. It could always be worse baby. You still here and you are beginning your life and you going to college. That's something a lot of people can never say. They ain't here to say it." Karma said, "I get that Ms. Gwen. I get what you are saying but why now? Why even come into my life? I was used to not having a daddy. Now I don't really need him." Ms. Gwen said, "You say, why now?" I say, "Why not now? Isn't now better than never? You only get two parents in life and you don't get to pick them. I know y'all think Ms. Gwen is gonna be around forever, but we all gotta go one day. Don't get me wrong, I ain't tryna go nowhere no time soon. I got plans for myself. You never know who you gonna need or when or why baby. Don't cut off your nose to spite your face. If this man can help you, let him. He is your blood." Karma listened but she still had so many unanswered questions, like,

"What happened to the money he had
been sending Ms. Gwen all these years?
And how was she sending him pictures
of her without even telling her about it?
And the fact that he has a daughter the
same age...**Anjinique**." Karma didn't
say anything else about it, she said,
"Okay Ms. Gwen", but she knew she
wasn't going to talk to Charlie or cash
his check. She got up to go to bed. Ms.
Gwen said ..."And baby, what's going
on with you and Todd?" Karma said,
"Todd is a punk." Ms. Gwen smiled
and said, "Ok, I ain't getting in that.
Y'all work it out. Ms. Gwen loves you
baby." Ms. Gwen went to her room.

Karma went to lie down and looked at
her phone. The screen read "10 missed
calls", they were all from Todd. She
turned the phone off and went to sleep.

At the club, Janeese and T-Bone sat at
the bar drinking waiting for her time to

go on stage. T-Bone was excited to see Janeese do her thing. When she got up to get dressed, he said, "Work it like I taught you baby." She looked at him and smiled, knowing that he had never taught her anything. T-Bone moved to another seat. He wanted to be front and center when she came out.

Janeese came onto the stage and worked the crowd trying to fill up her bucket. She came down to the front of the stage and saw T-Bone and a couple of other faces. The tips started to come in. When she bent down to the floor none other than slimy stuck a twenty dollar bill in her bustier. She quickly moved away from the front. As she was wrapping up her act, she saw a man in a business suit. He dropped something directly in the bucket.

She got dressed and was glad she had T-Bone waiting for her. He talked a lot of stuff all the way to the house. They were both tired. They went to bed, separately. As soon as Janeese lay down Karma said, "Hey J, How did it go tonight? Janeese responded, "It was kool, but Ol' slimy was there. He got a lot of nerve still coming in there after what he did to you." Karma said, "Don't worry about him. I'm working on a plan for him. More importantly, I need you to go to the clinic with me, so I can handle this situation before I focus on anything else. Janeese said, "You know I got you K." She added, "Oh, Mr. Business Suit was there too. He dropped this in the bucket. It was a small envelope. Karma said she would look at it in the morning. They said goodnight and dozed off.

10

A PRAYIN' WOMAN ?

In the morning, Ms. Gwen was rustling around in the kitchen. She prepared a big breakfast for her kids. Ms. Gwen had a pot of coffee brewing; fresh squeezed orange juice; bacon; sausage; eggs with cheese; cheese grits; hash browns; pancakes and biscuits. She wanted to have everybody's favorites. She added some fresh strawberries and yogurt to balance it all out. T-Bone was the first to make it to the kitchen. He smelled the bacon. He walked into the kitchen stretching and said, "Damn, Ms. Gwen you set it out this morning!" He started scratching himself. Ms. Gwen turned around and said, "Boy, if you don't take yo nasty ass in that bathroom and brush yo teeth and wash your face, you gon wish you did, as she lifted the extra fryin pan above her head. You ain't in prison no more. Ms. Gwen don't put up with all that they do at that prison of yours. Thought you knew." T-Bone said, "Yes Ms. Gwen, you know you ain't changed a bit." She said, "No way, not me. What you git is what you git, now git!" He ran to the bathroom before she laid that fryin pan on his head. It wouldn't have been the first time. The divas came in together and they all sat down at the table to eat. Right away T-Bone went to grab a biscuit. Ms. Gwen slapped his hand with the butcher knife.

She looked up at him and said, "We gone say the grace. Let us bow our heads." Ms. Gwen bowed her head and started praying;

Dear Lord,

I know you don't hear from me often, but I be real busy tryna raise these kids and keep them out of trouble. Lord you already know that and you know it ain't easy.. I wanna ask you to help me to watch over these children, even if they think they already grown. You know and I know, they ain't. So Father God, I come to you with a heavy heart and I know you feel my pain.

T-Bone, Karma and Janeese started looking at each other. They figured Ms. Gwen was trying to make up for lost time. But Lord, the food was getting cold.

She continued, anyway, Father God, I ain't here for all of that right now. I know that you know the sentiment of my heart. Please bless this food that

*we are about to receive for the
nourishment of our bodies. I ask that
you touch these kids and make 'em
know, like I know. I know I threw
down on this here breakfast and I
expect we best to be eating it. Lord
Father God, in all of your Holiness.
AMEN*

They all said together, AAAAMEN!
They enjoyed their family breakfast.
After breakfast, they cleaned up the
kitchen to give Ms. Gwen a break. T-
Bone took out the garbage. Ms. Gwen
had told T-Bone that she wanted to talk
to him later. Karma was feeling tired
and she knew she needed to hurry up
and deal with her situation. She went to
her room to lie down. She opened the
envelope that Michael had sent through
Janeese. Karma was wondering, "What
is up with this dude and why does he
keep leaving his card for me?" She
opened the envelope. The outside of

the envelope read, "Baby Girl". She looked at it and said to herself, "Baby Girl huh?" That's the same thing Charlie had called her. His envelope smelled so good, she wondered what cologne it was. She unfolded the letter.

Baby Girl, or should I say Ms. Mocha Latte or Peppa,

You are very mysterious, and I like it. I know you don't know me but I intend to change that very quickly.

I feel like I know you already. You are such a beautiful specimen on the outside but I want to see how beautiful you are inside. Will you allow me that opportunity? I promise I won't bite, unless you like that, ha,ha.

Seriously, I am a professional man as you can see by my card. There is something about you that I can't let get away and believe me I don't chase women because I don't have to.

I have been worried about you since the accident and I have missed you at the Club. You were really working the crowd that night, including me.

I am very interested in speaking with you and getting to know you better. Why don't we start with a cup of coffee so we can talk? Can you meet me at the Starbucks on Richards Street one day this week?

Please call me at the number below either way. I will respect your decision. You are the apple of my eye. I will be awaiting your call.

Until I can see you again,

Mike
Michael Buchanan, Esq.
1 (800) 332- 5567

Karma stared at the letter and said out loud, "What the hell?" Janeese said, "What? What?" She handed the letter to Janeese to read and laid back down. Janeese read the letter slowly. When she finished it she smelled the letter and said, "Damn girl, at least you know he smells good. He smells like a Reese's Cup or something." Karma looked at Janeese and shook her head. She said, Girl you are too silly. He don't smell like no damn Reese's Cup. He smell like a grown ass man." Janeese said, "Okay, okay, are you going to call him and meet him?"

Karma said, "I am not doin anything until we leave that clinic tomorrow and have everything taken care of. We need to be there early and I can't eat nuthin after midnight." Janeese asked, "Are you scared?" Karma said, "Naw, I ain't scared. I know this has to be done. I am hurt though. I feel so betrayed by everybody. This should be me and

Todd's"... she started crying. Janeese
came over to Karma's bed and gave her
a hug. Karma said, "Instead, I am in
this situation and I don't even know
how it happened or what all that freak
did to me. I want him dead and Imma
see that it happens or at least close to it."
Janeese said, "Are you sure of what you
are saying or are you just mad right
now?" I am working on my plan to take
care of Mr. Samuel's, Karma said. I'm
not gonna rush this because I want it to
be perfectly executed and on point. We
are gonna see who gets the last laugh."
"Janeese said, "Wow, you are really
serious." "Hell Yeah, said Karma,
wouldn't you be?" Janeese said, "I guess
I would."

The phone rang, it was Todd. Janeese
answered the phone. Karma was
waving her hands in the air, meaning
I'm not here. Janeese said, Hello?"
Todd said, "What's up J? Where is

Karma? I been tryna reach her for a couple of days. What is she on? Janeese repeated, "What is she on? Uh, she looked at Karma. Karma looked the other way. Janeese said again, "What is she on?' Todd said, "Yeah that's what I said. What's wrong with you? What is going on up there?" Janeese said, "Why don't you tell **me** what's going on?" Ain't nothin goin on with me," Todd said. She couldn't take it anymore, she said, "Well that ain't what the fuck we heard you raggedy ass fool. You are stupid as hell. Don't call here no more, because it ain't nobody here that wants to talk to you. Call skank ass Janet if you wanna talk. She hung up the phone. Janeese turned to Karma and said, "Sorry K. I couldn't hold it." Karma just shook her head but she didn't care anymore.

Todd stood starring at the phone. He thought to himself, "That damn Janet. I wish I knew what happened. I need to talk to Karma. I have to get back home and deal with Janet. I can't lose Karma. ...And definitely not for Janet. "

11

WORK THE PLAN

Ms. Gwen called T-Bone and told him they needed to sit down and have a talk. They went in the living room and sat down. Ms. Gwen said, "T-Bone, I need to hear what your plans are for your future. What are you going to do with yourself? You need to do something constructive. You need to find something to keep yourself busy so you don't get in any trouble. Have you given this any thought?" T-Bone said, "Damn, Ms. Gwen, I just got out. I just got home. You ridin me already. Naw, I ain't gave no thought to nothing yet. I am just tryna get used to not being locked up." Ms. Gwen told him, "Well let me help you with this baby. You will get up in the morning and start looking for a job. You will find out about getting you GED and You will NOT be living with Ms. Gwen come the end of August. When those two girls go to college it is time for Ms. Gwen. You feel me?" "Damn, you cold. I'm your son. How you just gone play me like that?" "Listen, you playin yo damn self. You about to be twenty-five, you are a man and I ain't taking care of no man. It's time for you to make it on your own. Make some plans. Now, if my plan don't work for you, you can always use the Two Foot Rule baby," said Ms. Gwen. "Yeah, what's the Two Foot Rule, Ms. Gwen?" She said, "If you ain't happy with my plan and you can't contribute to the plan...then you can use yo two feet and walk yo happy ass right out the damn door. That's the Rule!" T-Bone got up and walked away. He wasn't trying to hear what Ms. Gwen was talking about today. He went to hang out with some of his old friends. Ms. Gwen just shook her head. He was starting out the wrong way and however it ended up was up to him. All she could do was pray for him and let go and let God. It was out of her hands. She knew what hanging out in the street and drinking all hours of the night would get him but it was his life. She got ready for bed. Ms. Gwen lay in her bed for a few minutes thinking. She got back up and got down on her knees.

God,

I know I'm coming to you twice in one day and I know you ain't used to that. But I feel like Imma really need your help with this boychild. If you can touch him Lord, just touch him. I'm giving it to you.

She got up and got back in the bed.

12

IT'S NO LONGER A SITUATION

The next morning the girls were up early and out the door. Karma had an appointment that couldn't be missed. As Karma and Janeese were walking out of the door, in walked T-Bone. He had been out all night and he reeked of alcohol and maybe something else. They made it to the clinic and had to wait for a while. Karma was anxious to get it over, and even more to get any trace of slimy out of her system. Karma said she wasn't scared, but the longer she had to wait, the harder it was getting for her to think about anything else. Janeese brought magazines and candy, so she was preoccupied. Karma had no choice but to think to herself. She had all kinds of thoughts running through her mind.

She went from Janet to Charlie, in her mind. She wanted to inflict bodily harm on Janet but she realized that Todd was responsible for that mess. The best way to hurt Todd was to never speak to him again. She didn't care if it hurt her too. She would never speak to him again. Things were still strained with Ms. Gwen but she decided not to worry about that now. Slimy would have his day in court as soon as she finalized her plan. Charlie had hurt her so deeply by not being in her life. She had dealt with it already. She wondered,"Why is he adding insult to injury?" Karma felt that she couldn't deal with Charlie and this **Anjinique** issue made her feel even worse. "He was in her life but not mine, she thought." What nerve. That's one of the reasons she was at the clinic. She would never want to have a child without a father.

She decided to take a chance on Michael. She would meet him for coffee as soon as she got past this situation. She heard someone say, "Karma Anderson". She rose slowly and walked toward the voice. She listened to the instructions and went in the changing room. Janeese was standing right next to her looking like she was about to cry. Karma said, "Girl you know Ms. Gwen will know you are crying. It doesn't matter where you are. Now, suck it up." They hugged each other for an extended period of time. Karma walked away to get it done.

Janeese returned to her seat and her candy bar. It seemed like she had been sitting there for days. She was so nervous. She had gone to the nurse's station five times already. It had only been an hour in reality. Karma walked out from a back room. She was moving slowly and Janeese didn't know what to do but she wanted to do something. She said, "Let me carry your purse." Karma said, "I'm okay. You know what I t

thought about while I was waiting to go
in?" "What?" asked Janeese. "We have
not gotten our college letters yet. We
need to watch for them so we will know
where we are going," she said. Janeese
said, "Yep."

When they got home Ms. Gwen was
out. Karma went to lie down and
Janeese went to make her a cup of tea.
Janeese brought the tea and asked, "Can
I get anything else for you? You want
some chocolate?" Karma squeezed a
smile out and said, "You really think
candy cures everything, don't you?
Janeese said, "Works for me."Karma
said, "Just give me a couple pain pills
please." Janeese gave her the pills and
they both took a nap.

Janeese woke up when she heard a
rustling noise in the room. When she sat
up she saw T-Bone walking out of the

room. She called him, "T-Bone?" He stuck his head back in the room. She asked him, "Did you just leave out of here?" He said, "Uh, yeah baby, I was looking for you, but I saw that you was sleep." She said, "Oh, okay. Are you going to the club with me tonight?" he said, "I wouldn't miss it cutie pie. What time we leaving?" She smiled and said, "Ten".

T-Bone left the house and Janeese watched television while Karma slept. At 9pm the alarm went off, Janeese got up to take her shower and Karma woke up. Janeese asked her how she felt. Karma said, "I'm okay, I think I will go with you. I need to get out of the house for a while." "Are you sure that's okay?" asked Janeese. "Yeah, I will be okay." Karma got up and got dressed too.

They heard Ms. Gwen walking in humming. She sounded happy.

It was about a quarter to ten when T-Bone came back home. Janeese said, "We are leaving in fifteen minutes. I told you ten o'clock." T-Bone was looking a little crazy, he said, "No worries, I can be ready in ten minutes." T-Bone was ready in ten minutes. He changed his clothes but he didn't wash up. He was acting kind of strange.

When we got to the club, Leon was rushing me to get dressed and get on stage. A lot of the girls had been leaving Leon's. We had heard that there was a new club opening up on the other side of town. I went to get dressed and Karma and T-Bone went to get their seats.

Karma had a ginger ale on the rocks and T-Bone was ordering tequila shots. He was acting weird. While Karma was seated the waitress brought her another ginger ale. The waitress said, 'From the gentleman in the suit."

Karma turned around and it was Michael. He walked toward her and asked how she was doing and if she had gotten his note. She said she was fine and that she had gotten the note. He asked her if she would meet him for coffee to talk, and she agreed. Janeese came on stage and Michael left. He was only there looking for Karma.

T-Bone was hanging at the bar with some guys as if he knew them and he was buying tequila shots for everyone. Janeese did her thing and got dressed. They all sat at the bar. Janeese ordered a Jack and Coke. Karma stuck with the ginger ale and T-Bone continued to drink tequila shots. He appeared to be tipsy but he was still laughing and talking with his friends.

Someone walked up behind Karma and hugged her from behind. She turned around and it was slimy.

She told him he should walk away if he knew what was good. He said, "Yeah baby I know what's good. You are." He started laughing. Karma stood up but she remembered about her procedure earlier that day. T-Bone heard the commotion and came over. He said, "Is everything okay, Karma?" Mr. Samuel's said, "Yeah it's okay. Just a lover's quarrel.

" T-Bone said, "Hey man, I wasn't talking to you. I said Karma." Mr. Samuel's said, "I was talking to you." T-Bone swung and hit Mr. Samuel's dead in the mouth. He hit him so hard his front tooth fell out. Security ran over to break it up. They escorted Mr. Samuel's to the door. He said, "I don't think you wanted to do that." T-Bone said, "Oh yeah I did exactly what the hell I meant to do," T-Bone was spitting as he was talking. Mr. Samuel's was gone. The girls finished their drinks and got ready to go home. Janeese was concerned about Karma being out too long.

As the three of them walked out, Mr. Samuel's jumped out from around the building with a tire iron in his hand. He swung at T-Bone. T-Bone was already intoxicated after all of the tequila shots that he had. He said, "Hey man, you really need to step off. You got the wrong dude tonight." He clapped his hands together and said, "Real talk." Mr. Samuel's swung the tire iron and hit T-Bone right across his face. T-Bone lost all of his control. He reached inside of his jacket and pulled out a long knife. He stuck the knife in Mr. Samuel's side and then turned it. He looked him in the eye and said, "What I tell you punk? You want some more?" T-Bone started jumping around wildly. He was pumped. Mr. Samuel's fell to the ground and blood gushed from his side. Janeese said, "Let's get out of here."

Karma looked at Mr. Samuel's lying on the ground and placed her high heeled pump in the center of his chest. She bent down and spit in his face. She whispered in his ear, "Karma is a Bitch". T-Bone got excited when he saw what his sister had done. He turned around and stabbed Mr. Samuel's in the leg several times. T-Bone laughed and said, "Karma is a Bitch, ain't she?" Ha-ha. He didn't even know how true his statement was. For good measure, he sliced Mr. Samuel's face three times in the shape of a "K". Janeese started crying, "Let's get out of here." The three of them left just as the security guards were coming to the parking lot. When they got home, T-Bone was covered in blood.

Janeese was hysterical and she woke Ms. Gwen up with her crying. Ms. Gwen ran to see what was going on. She saw T-Bone's clothes and he was still holding the bloody knife in his hand.

Ms. Gwen didn't even want to know the details, she immediately dropped to the floor.

Lord,

I have faith in you and I know you know what is best in every situation. I have lifted my hands of this situation and it is now yours to see through. I trust you Lord.

Ms. Gwen hugged her son one last time and said, "Well, I guess you chose the Two Foot Plan. Get ready. Your ride will be here shortly." She knew it wouldn't be long before the police arrived. She also knew that T-Bone would have a new residence for a very long time.

Janeese was crying and laying on the floor she was in shock at what had happened.

Karma on the other hand was calm. It wasn't the plan that she was working on for Mr. Samuel's, but it would do. Karma went to her room to lie down. It had been a long day and she needed her rest.

Ms. Gwen told Janeese, "Baby come in here with Ms. Gwen." She let Janeese lie in her bed until she calmed down and she gave her a miniature snickers.

T-Bone sat on the couch and waited for his fate to arrive. By the time the police got there, T-Bone had taken a long, hot bubble bath. He knew where he was going he wouldn't see another bath for a long time. The officers knew T-Bone from when he was growing up in the neighborhood. He was always in some kind of trouble. T-Bone had been guilty of everything from stealing the neighbor's cat to, well…now this.

KARMA

Ms. Gwen came out of her room to see her child taken away in handcuffs one last time. She asked the officers, who she knew, "What is the charge?" One officer turned to Ms. Gwen and said, "Ms. Gwen, we don't know what all of the charges will be. We don't know the condition of the victim or if he will survive. The charges may be upgraded later." Ms. Gwen said, "Well can I help you with that? " The officers looked at each other curiously, but they did have a history with Ms. Gwen so they knew anything could come out of her mouth. The officer humored her, he said, "Yes Ms. Gwen go ahead and help us with this charge. " They waited. Ms. Gwen said, "I know I birthed this child, but it seems to me that he is guilty as hell. He is guilty of **DUMBASSORY** and everybody knows that it is a felony in every state. He don't listen and now he has to learn." She reached over to give T-Bone a hug as they took him out. He pulled away from her. He didn't get a chance to say goodbye to the girls.

In the police car on the ride to the station, all he could think about is how bad he felt for not listening to Ms. Gwen and her damn Two Foot Rule. If only he had not gotten mad at her. He realized now that he could've stopped to listen to some of what she was saying. He was also upset with himself for catching up with his old friends from the neighborhood. T-Bone knew he couldn't handle liquor and drugs, and well, that's why he was taking this ride today. "Just stupid," he thought to himself. He tried to hit himself in the head but he had the handcuffs on and couldn't lift his hands high enough. He was not upset about beating Mr. Samuel's down. He felt he shouldn't have been poppin off. He didn't even know that he was the one that had hurt his sister (Karma is a bitch). What hurt his heart the most was yet to be revealed, but he knew he could never forgive himself for it.

At the house, the girls were up and Ms. Gwen was explaining that the police had picked T-Bone up and taken him in. She told them that they didn't know if Mr. Samuel's was dead or alive. Janeese was so nervous about it. Karma felt bad for T-Bone, but she didn't really care if Mr. Samuel's was dead, as a matter of fact she felt he deserved it. It was a sad situation but Ms. Gwen summed it up. She told them, "T-Bone had just as many chances as the two of you. He just didn't use them wisely. Life is about choices…and he chose to be a damn fool and guess what? He was damn good at it. So, don't feel bad for him. He is a successful person. He decided to be an asshole and he succeeded. As if it wasn't enough assholes already in the world. He could've been a doctor or a lawyer, but it was his choice. Life goes on."

When Ms. Gwen said, "lawyer" Karma remembered she was supposed to meet with Michael at Starbucks. She didn't want to stick around the house acting sick. She was glad that the situation that she had was over. She planned to meet Michael and find out what he wanted so badly.

Janeese decided to catch up with Carlos today and cool out. They went back to the room to get ready for the day.

In all of the excitement that happened, Janeese had forgotten to count her tips from the night before. She pulled out the bucket and she only had about $1,000. Tips had been declining since the new club had opened and Karma had been off. She looked at Karma and said, "Damn all I got was $980 for last night." Karma said, "That's kool, we still have a few more weeks. Add it to the college fund box. We are in good shape." Janeese went to the hiding place to add the money. The box was gone. Janeese said, "Karma, did you move the box?"

Karma said, "No Janeese, it's in the same spot." Janeese felt on the shelf but all she felt was dust and a piece of paper. She grabbed the piece of paper and dusted her hand off. When she looked down at her hand, she saw the check from Charlie. Karma said, "Do you see it?" Janeese stood there like she had seen a ghost. She read, "Payable to Karma Marie Anderson, Five thousand dollars, My Baby Girl." Janeese seemed to be in a trance. Karma said, "Janeese, JANEESE", "What the hell are you doing?" Janeese snapped out of it and held the check up in the air and said, "This is all that is in the closet, this, and a whole bunch of dust." Karma ran to the closet and tore it up. She searched high and she searched low. She started throwing shoes and clothes out of the closet door. She was sweating and scratching her head. She sat on the closet floor and began to cry quietly. She couldn't let Ms. Gwen hear her. Janeese turned the television up. Ms. Gwen could not catch them crying and she couldn't know about the money because of how they earned it. Janeese said, "T-Bone." Karma said, "That damn T-Bone." Janeese told Karma that she had seen him sneaking out of the room the day before when they were napping. She told her about his excuse for being in the room. It was all starting to come together. T-Bone was buying drinks for people at the club and acting really strange and he had a knife on him. "Could he have spent the entire $20,000?" Janeese asked? Karma said, "It doesn't matter if he spent it or not. He took it. It's gone and we are screwed." Karma thought to herself, "Betrayed again. Who can you trust?"

At that moment, Ms. Gwen tapped on the door and said, "Todd is on this damn phone again. Are you going to talk to him or not?" They both screamed in unison, **"NO!"** They could hear Ms. Gwen telling Todd, "I'm sorry baby but ain't neither one of 'em trying

Candy Ain't Always Sweet Page 174

to talk to you. I don't know what you did this time baby, but it must be pretty bad if Janeese won't even talk to you. You better fix it, but I ain't getting involved in that honey. Make it do what it do." Todd sounded like he had lost his best friend. He said, "Thanks Ms. Gwen."

Ms. Gwen yelled to the girls, "Y'all got some mail out here." They were still so distraught over the money they weren't in any hurry to see any mail. Karma told Janeese, "We will think of something." Janeese sat on the floor eating Reese's Pieces. Karma remembered her date with Michael. She went to the bathroom to get showered.

13

A REAL MAN

Karma went to the Starbuck's on Richard Street to see what he wanted. He was there when she walked in and he was watching her every move. Karma loved an audience, especially an audience as fine as this man was. Karma went into immediate Naomi Campbell walk, to give him something to look at, since he was looking. He seemed to be enjoying what he saw. She walked up to the table and he jumped up and pulled her chair out. At that moment she got a whiff of his cologne. The cologne smelled so delicious on him, she felt her knees buckle just a bit. She sat down before she fell. He pushed her seat in and ever so gently, stroked the back of her neck. He smiled as he took his seat and said, "I am so glad you decided to join me. I have been waiting for this opportunity for some time." Karma said, "It's just coffee." He said, "Oh but it's so much more than that. You don't realize it now, but you will soon, very soon." Karma thought that he was so damn sexy and his voice alone would make a woman drop to her knees. She blushed and asked him, "What kind of cologne are you wearing?" He replied, "It's called, "Fierce" by Abercrombie and Fitch." Karma repeated after him, "Fierce" by Abercrombie and Fitch...I see." She was so taken by his demeanor. He reached for her hand and said, "What can I get for you, sweetie?" She had forgotten for a minute that they were in Starbuck's. She said, "Oh, I will have a Grande White Chocolate Mocha, Skim, No whip please." He smiled, and damn he had some pretty teeth. He said, "That's funny, I would've thought you would have ordered the Mocha Latte." He added, "I will get that. I think that is exactly what I want...MOCHA LATTE."

KARMA

She smiled. She picked up on what he was trying to say since her stage name was Ms. Mocha Latte. Karma was intrigued by him. She watched him as he went to the counter to place the order. She noticed that she wasn't the only one watching him either. Several women in the coffee shop had their eyes on him. Karma thought with a smirk on her face, "Too bad for them, he is with me." Karma was thinking about everything that had happened recently and was really not ready to jump into anything. She said to herself, "I will just see what he is talking about. I am about to leave for school soon anyway." Michael returned to the table with the drinks and took his seat. He was immaculately dressed and he looked very professional. Karma was a little intimidated by it. She had never had a real man. She had only dated Todd who had betrayed her. She had the incident with Mr. Samuel's. She didn't even remember what happened to her. The only experience she had had with men had been the men at the club, T-Bone and well, Charlie. Her past didn't say much for men. Michael looked into her eyes when he spoke. Karma kept looking away. She felt like she was melting when he did that. She felt that he could see straight through her. He said, "Allow me to introduce myself...I am Michael T. Buchanan, Esq. I have my own law practice which was passed down to me when my dad died.

I am a serious businessman, but I like to have fun. I am looking for someone to enjoy the good life with. You have caught my eye and I want to get to know you better. What is your real name?" She hesitated, and then said, "My name is Karma." He said, "Karma," that is an interesting name. They talked some more about Karma's plans for her future. She told him about her plans to leave for college in a few weeks and that she wanted to major in Business. She told him about Janeese and Ms. Gwen but she stopped short on that topic. She didn't want to tell him too much about Ms. Gwen. She didn't want to scare him away. Michael told Karma about his latest business venture. He had opened a night club with live entertainment, and it was called, "Club Excite." Karma had heard about the new club opening and she knew that a lot of the girls had left Leon's to go and work at Club Excite. Michael told Karma about the big Grand Opening celebration that he was having on the weekend and he would love for her to be his date. He told her to invite Janeese also. He would have a car come to pick them up. Karma agreed. Michael had another appointment and needed to cut the coffee break short. He stood and kissed Karma on the cheek. His lips felt so soft on her face. Karma melted in her chair, she just sat there for another fifteen minutes thinking about the conversation and smelling his "Fierce" on her cheek.

When she snapped out of it, she hurried home to tell Janeese all about Michael T. Buchannan, Esq.

14

WE GOIN' TO COLLEGE

When Karma walked in the house, Ms. Gwen said, "I guess y'all don't care about mail. It's in there on the kitchen table." Karma said, "Okay Ms. Gwen." She grabbed the stack of mail and took it to their room. Janeese was in the room watching the *Lifetime Movie Network*. She was crying and eating bon bon's. Karma said, "Janeese, What the hell?" Janeese said, "I know, it's just so sad." She was referring to the movie that she was watching. She grabbed more tissue and blew her nose. Karma said, 'You need to pull it together sister. Life is passing you by." Janeese said, "Oh Lord, you are starting to sound like Ms. Gwen."

Karma was excited, she told Janeese about her date with Michael and about the grand opening at Club Excite. Janeese was excited too. She sat up in the bed and said, "We need new outfits." Karma said, "Shopping Trip". They remembered they only had the $980 from Janeese's last performance. They agreed they could make it work. They got ready to leave for the mall and Karma remembered the mail that Ms. Gwen had been buggin about. She said, "Janeese this is for you and these are for me." Janeese opened her letter first. It read:

Dear Ms. Block:

Let me congratulate you on the behalf of the University!

*You have been selected for admission in the program of **Culinary Arts** for the fall semester of 2011. Your academic profile talks about your commitment and interest in academics. We are sure you will* *prove your mettle and not let our confidence down.*

Enclosed herewith your letter, you will find your rooming assignment:

You will be roommates with:

Karma Anderson

This assignment was made at your mutual request. Additional dormitory information will be sent under separate cover.

The entire University welcomes you and wishes you all the best for your career. We appreciate your enthusiasm in our university and hope all your wishes are fulfilled by us.

Yours truly,

Freshman Admissions

Janeese read the letter out loud, all the way through the part about Karma Anderson. After she read that part she just started screaming.

Karma ripped her envelope open and started reading. It read the same except for the concentration which read, *Business Administration.* They both started screaming at their highest pitch and jumping on and off the bed. Ms. Gwen came into the room to see what was going on. Karma handed her the letter and she started screaming too. They were all so excited. This went on until they were too tired to move. They lay on the bed for a few minutes just smiling and thinking about their respective futures.

Karma sat up and looked at the other letter that she had. It was from Todd. Karma tossed it to the side and said, "Let's go shopping." They left for the mall.

On the night of the grand opening, the girls were dressed and looking absolutely beautiful. Ms. Gwen said, "Come here, let me look at you." They came and modeled their outfits for Ms. Gwen. They were so happy and excited about the prospects for their future. Ms. Gwen said, "Okay, y'all ain't half bad, but in Ms. Gwen's day, baay bee, I could shole work a crowd. Just give me some four inch heels and any ol' piece of rag. It ain't the clothes that make you baby. You make the clothes." She said, "Shit, truth be told, Ms. Gwen still got it." She started dancing around and went down to the floor. While she was down there bouncing around, she told the girls, "Ms. Gwen can still drop it like it's hot chile." They watched her for a few minutes bouncing around down there. Ms. Gwen said, "Yeaaah, I can drop it like it's hot, but I just need a little help bringing it back up. C'mon over here and help Ms. Gwen baby.

Don't just stand there looking." The girls laughed hysterically as each one took an arm and helped her up. They sat her on the couch where she had one hand on her back and the other on her leg. Ms. Gwen had to laugh at herself after that one.

15

"CLUB EXCITE"

The doorbell rang. The car that Michael sent had arrived. They grabbed their purses and headed for the door. They said, "Goodnight Ms. Gwen. Don't wait up." Ms. Gwen said, "Y'all have fun." She went to look for some Epsom salt to soak in a hot tub of water.

When the car pulled up to the venue, there was a huge neon sign that said, *"Club Excite - Where the Fun Begins."* Everything was so fabulous looking, the lights, the waitresses, the valet. Karma and Janeese were really impressed.

They have never been exposed to this side of life. As soon as they entered the room, they were escorted to the VIP lounge, where Michael eagerly awaited their arrival. Michael stood up and walked toward Karma. He gave her a hug and held it for a while. He turned her around to check out what she was wearing. Karma had selected a black strapless dress that fit every curve of her body and a five inch black pump that made her look very sexy. Michael took it all in and said to Karma, "Girl, you are going to hurt somebody in here tonight." He introduced himself to Janeese, and kissed her hand. Janeese giggled. They were escorted to their table and the champagne was served. Throughout the night, Michael would sneak kisses on Karma's face and neck. They watched the performer's and saw some of the girls who used to work at Leon's. The club was twice the size of Leon's and everything was brand new. It was very impressive.

Janeese wanted to be performing that night. Karma didn't. She wanted to be right where she was, in Michael's arms. Karma wished that the night would never end. The car took them back home after the club closed for the night.

Karma remembered the letter from Todd that she had tossed on the bed before leaving. She would read it tomorrow. She really wasn't interested in what Todd had to say, especially now that she had Michael in her life. Michael Buchanan was a real man. It was the first time that Karma had ever met one.

In the morning, Ms. Gwen was up, but moving slow. She was in the kitchen trying to prepare a little breakfast. The girls snickered at her hobbling around the kitchen. Karma said to Ms. Gwen,

"You might want to stick to dropping the eggs like they are hot, instead of your body." Janeese fell out laughing and said, "Please pass me the pancakes." Ms. Gwen didn't dignify their teasing with a response. She got her cup of coffee and eased into her chair. She said, "Karma, that damn Todd called all night. I could hardly sleep." Karma sighed and ignored the comment. She was so enthralled with Michael, she wanted to say, "Todd who?" When breakfast was over and the kitchen was clean, the girls retreated to their room. Janeese turned on the television to find a good movie. Karma opened Todd's letter and began to read.

Dear Karma,

Before I even start this, I have to say I am so sorry everything went down the way it did. I know I should never have gotten involved with Janet. I never had any feelings for her. I was just kicking it with her to fill the time. You are the only one that I love and I don't know how I will make it without you.

I know that I should have told you that she was pregnant and I did try but I couldn't bring it out.

I didn't want to risk hurting you by telling you that. I was hoping to make it go away. I tried to get her to get an abortion but she refused.

She is supposed to put the baby up for adoption. Hell, Karma I don't even know if the baby is mine. Everybody knows how Janet is and I only slept with her one time. I guess I am the sucker for doing that. I know I crossed the line and I can only pray that you will consider taking me back one day.

Karma, you know that we have shared our inner most thoughts and feelings with each other and we have a special bond for life.

I am hurting really bad right now without you in my life and I want to be there for you with Charlie and everything.

I know you will be getting ready to go to college by the time I come back. I hope to see you before you go. I will be going as well. I don't even know which college you are going to. If I miss you I will send a letter to Ms. Gwen to get your information.

Remember that we will be together no matter what, when it's all said and done.

You will forever have my heart!

Love Todd

Karma laid the letter down on her bed and thought for a minute. She decided that with all that had happened she would just leave the past behind her. The past included; Todd, T-Bone, Mr. Samuel's and Charlie. Karma was focused on her future. Her future included: going to college, Janeese, Ms. Gwen and of course Michael.

16

DUMBASSORY IS A FELONY

Ms. Gwen went to court for the sentencing of her only son. Tyrone Anderson (T-Bone). Ms. Gwen was sad but she knew that she had given him the best advice that she could and had surrendered him to God. She sat there waiting to hear the final judgment. She looked across the aisle and there was his trifling ass daddy, Tyrone with his broke down wife. Ms. Gwen wondered to herself, "Where was his raggedy ass when the boy needed him?"

Tyrone stood up in the black suit and tie that Ms. Gwen had sent for him to wear. He faced the judge to receive his fate.

KARMA

As it turned out, T-Bone got fifty years to life. As a repeat offender, it would be a long time before he would be free again. Ms. Gwen thought, "That's not so bad. Now he won't have to make any choices. They will all be made for him."

Mr. Samuel's didn't die, much to Karma's disappointment. However, he had severe liver damage. He would not be able to teach anymore and would walk with a limp for the rest of his life. Karma was satisfied with the fact that he would have a constant reminder of the mistake he made.

17

MS. GWEN'S PICNIC

There were just a couple more days before the girls left for college. Ms. Gwen had planned a huge picnic in the park. She wanted everyone to celebrate in the happiness that she felt for her girls. Karma was the first person in Anderson history to even visit a college, let alone to be enrolled. Now Ms. Gwen couldn't wait until she graduated from college. That would be her new focus, well maybe she could find a couple other things to focus on in the meantime. At the picnic, Ms. Gwen had her famous pies and cakes and all of the barbecue fixings. All of the neighborhood people were there. Janeese was there with Carlos. Karma was there with Michael.

Michael had arranged for a jumping gym for all of the little kids and he had snow cones for them. Ms. Gwen was there with Principal Andrews, from grammar school. Janeese and Karma were in shock. Principal Andrews came over and congratulated them both on their accomplishments. The girls pulled Ms. Gwen to the side and wanted to know how long had this been going on? How did she keep this secret? They had so many questions. Ms. Gwen called her man over and wrapped her arm around his neck. She said, "Baby, they want to know how we kept our secret." Principal Andrews just smiled and blushed. It was clear that Ms. Gwen was the aggressor in the relationship. She kissed him on the lips in front of everybody and said, "Baby I might not drop it like it's hot, but I shole got my mojo workin now." Everybody laughed so hard they almost lost their plates. Ms. Gwen called everyone to come close for her final remarks:

I would like to thank all of y'all for coming and sharing in my joy and happiness. I didn't know if I would ever see the day but baay bee, my girls are GOIN TO COLLEGE and I will be going to the college to check on my girls too.

Karma and Janeese rolled their eyes up in their head.

Ms. Gwen ain't raise no fools' honey. She stopped for a second and thought about T-Bone. She thought to herself, "Well maybe one."

*She said, "Well 50/50 ain't bad. Guess what else chile, Ms. Gwen know that Candy Ain't Always Sweet but this time I got me a pixie honey. Gourmet Chocolate with caramel and **NUTS!** Hell-o! See y'all at the college.*

Now that you know the family, what could possibly happen when Karma and Janeese go to college?

Two experienced strippers, grown ass women prepare to set the campus on fire and anyone who gets in their way.

What drama could Ms. Gwen get into with the girls away?

Look for Charlie, Anjinique and Todd in the next edition.

Chile, y'all betta stay tuned, Ms. Gwen will whip that ass.

Karma & Janeese
College Ain't Ready!

This author can be contacted at
Papillonbooks@att.net

Follow on Twitter@papillonbooks

Blog
"I Think Therefore, I Blog."
Butterfliesarefreeandme@blogspot.com

"Change is the essence of life. Be willing to surrender what you are for what you could become."

Discussion Questions

1. Other than the most obvious reason, why do you think Karma was so angry with Charlie?

2. Do you feel that Karma gave up on Todd?

3. What are the life lessons that Ms. Gwen tried to teach, in her own way?

4. Do you think Janet's baby was really Todd's?

5. Do you think Karma's baby was really Mr. Samuel's?

6. In your opinion, did Ms. Gwen give up on T-Bone?

7. Why do you think Karma assumed that Charlie played an active role in Anjinique's life?

8. Do you think that Karma will ever accept Charlie and Anjinique as a part of her life?

Made in the USA
Middletown, DE
07 April 2022